LEVELED
Readers'
Theater

Grade 1

Editorial Development: De Gibbs
Lisa Vitarisi Mathews
Ann Rossi
Copy Editing: Carrie Gwynne
Art Direction: Cheryl Puckett
Kathy Kopp
Illustration: Cheryl Nobens
Cover Design: David Price
Design/Production: Arynne Elfenbein
Yuki Meyer
Marcia Smith

EMC 3481

Evan-Moor
EDUCATIONAL PUBLISHERS®
Helping Children Learn since 1979

Congratulations on your purchase of some of the finest teaching materials in the world.

Photocopying the pages in this book is permitted for single-classroom use only. Making photocopies for additional classes or schools is prohibited.

For information about other Evan-Moor products, call 1-800-777-4362, fax 1-800-777-4332, or visit our Web site, www.evan-moor.com. Entire contents © 2009 EVAN-MOOR CORP. 18 Lower Ragsdale Drive, Monterey, CA 93940-5746. Printed in USA.

Correlated
to State Standards

Visit *teaching-standards.com* to view a correlation of this book's activities to your state's standards. This is a free service.

Contents

Introduction

Scripts and Activities

LEVELS

Answer Key

What's in Every Unit?

1 A teacher resource page guides instruction.

Offers suggestions for introducing the topic and activating students' prior knowledge

Differentiates reading parts as above, on, or below grade level

Includes suggestions and examples for making vocabulary more accessible

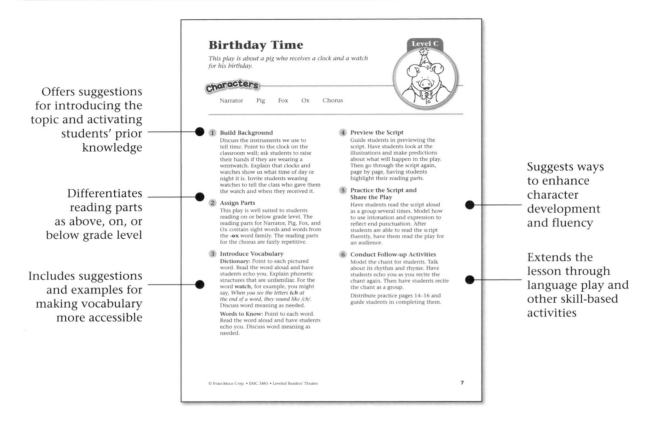

Suggests ways to enhance character development and fluency

Extends the lesson through language play and other skill-based activities

2 A reproducible dictionary page introduces vocabulary from the script.

Provides students with visual cues to connect key words and meanings

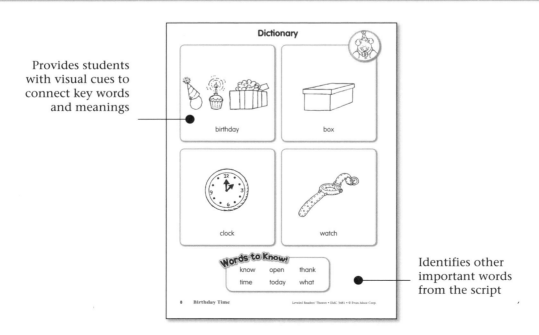

Identifies other important words from the script

3 A reproducible minibook script is designed especially for students in the primary grades.

Easy assembly:
• Reproduce script pages.
• Cut along dotted lines.
• Staple into a minibook.

Illustrations support comprehension.

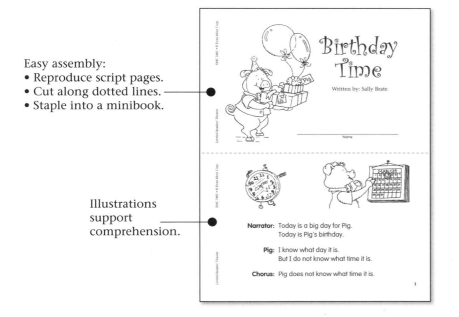

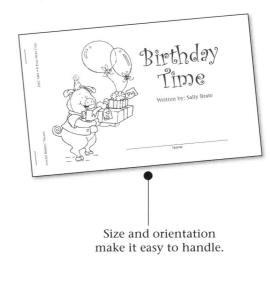

Size and orientation make it easy to handle.

4 A reproducible chant provides additional fluency practice.

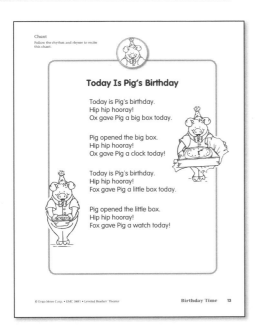

5 Reproducible activity pages reinforce vocabulary and comprehension.

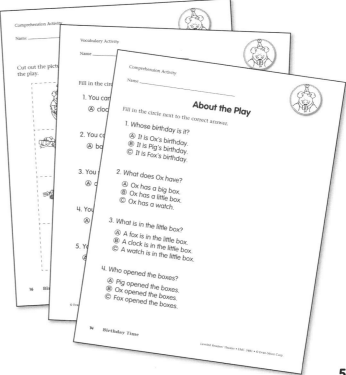

Using the Leveled Scripts to Increase Reading Fluency

The National Reading Panel identifies fluency as a key component of reading instruction because of its impact on students' reading efficacy and comprehension. The *Leveled Readers' Theater* format provides a platform for fun, repeated readings that build students' reading fluency.

About the Reading Levels

Each play has been assigned a Guided Reading level (C–H) based on factors related to accessibility. The factors considered in leveling the scripts are:

- Text structure, such as plot, cause/effect, and problem/solution
- Text features, such as repetition, point of view, and dialogue
- Vocabulary
- Sentence complexity
- Illustration to text match
- Book and print features
- Genre and topic

Enhance Your Core Reading Program

You can use the leveled scripts as a supplement to your core reading program. The scripts provide a motivating resource that offers purposeful reading practice for students at many different reading levels. Assemble reading groups that include a range of ability levels so that more skilled readers can model fluency to less skilled readers. The engaging, relevant topics in *Leveled Readers' Theater* scripts will entertain and interest reluctant readers and provide fluent readers with the opportunity to explore and enjoy a variety of genres and characters.

Support English Language Learners

The *Leveled Readers' Theater* scripts provide a reading experience that can increase confidence and transform English Language Learners into fluent readers. The teacher resource pages and follow-up activities that accompany every unit provide the necessary support and scaffolding for effective instruction to EL students in the areas of reading, writing, listening, and speaking.

How to Present a Unit

Choose a leveled script that contains reading parts written at students' instructional reading levels. Use the teacher resource page to conduct guided instruction lessons that help students understand the topic and become comfortable with the format of the script. Start slowly and engage students in repeated readings, modeling fluency often, so that students gain confidence reading the script aloud. Support students by modeling reading strategies, such as using context clues, identifying word structure, and identifying letter-sound relationships. Use the follow-up vocabulary and comprehension activity pages as informal assessments to gauge students' understanding of the play.

Birthday Time

This play is about a pig who receives a clock and a watch for his birthday.

Narrator   Pig   Fox   Ox   Chorus

---

1 **Build Background**

Discuss the instruments we use to tell time. Point to the clock on the classroom wall; ask students to raise their hands if they are wearing a wristwatch. Explain that clocks and watches show us what time of day or night it is. Invite students wearing watches to tell the class who gave them the watch and when they received it.

2 **Assign Parts**

This play is well suited to students reading on or below grade level. The reading parts for the narrator, Pig, Fox, and Ox contain sight words and words from the **-ox** word family. The reading parts for the chorus are fairly repetitive.

3 **Introduce Vocabulary**

Dictionary: Point to each pictured word. Read the word aloud and have students echo you. Explain phonetic structures that are unfamiliar. For the word **watch**, for example, you might say, *When you see the letters **tch** at the end of a word, they sound like /ch/.* Discuss word meaning as needed.

Words to Know: Point to each word. Read the word aloud and have students echo you. Discuss word meaning as needed.

4 **Preview the Script**

Guide students in previewing the script. Have students look at the illustrations and make predictions about what will happen in the play. Then go through the script again, page by page, having students highlight their reading parts.

5 **Practice the Script and Share the Play**

Have students read the script aloud as a group several times. Model how to use intonation and expression to reflect end punctuation. After students are able to read the script fluently, have them read the play for an audience.

6 **Conduct Follow-up Activities**

Model the chant for students. Talk about its rhythm and rhyme. Have students echo you as you recite the chant again. Then have students recite the chant as a group.

Distribute practice pages 14–16 and guide students in completing them.

Dictionary

birthday

box

clock

watch

Words to Know!

know	open	thank
time	today	what

EMC 3481 • © Evan-Moor Corp.

Birthday Time

Written by: Sally Brate

_____
Name

EMC 3481 • © Evan-Moor Corp.

Narrator: Today is a big day for Pig.
Today is Pig's birthday.

Pig: I know what day it is.
But I do not know what time it is.

Chorus: Pig does not know what time it is.

1

Narrator: Ox came to see Pig.
Ox had a big box.

Ox: Happy birthday, Pig!
This big box is for you.

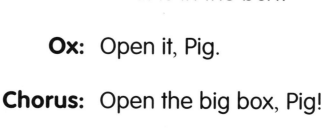

Pig: Thank you, Ox.
What is in the box?

Ox: Open it, Pig.

Chorus: Open the big box, Pig!

EMC 3481 • © Evan-Moor Corp.

Leveled Readers' Theater

Pig: A clock is in this box!

Ox: You can tell time with a clock.

Chorus: A clock was in the box from Ox.

4

Narrator: Fox came to see Pig.
Fox had a little box.

Fox: Happy birthday, Pig!
This little box is for you.

5

Pig: Thank you, Fox.
What is in the box?

Fox: Open it, Pig.

Chorus: Open the little box, Pig!

Pig: A watch is in this box!

Fox: You can tell time with a watch.

Chorus: A watch was in the box from Fox.
Now Pig has a clock and a watch.
Now Pig knows what time it is.

Chant

Follow the rhythm and rhyme to recite this chant.

Today Is Pig's Birthday

Today is Pig's birthday.
Hip hip hooray!
Ox gave Pig a big box today.

Pig opened the big box.
Hip hip hooray!
Ox gave Pig a clock today!

Today is Pig's birthday.
Hip hip hooray!
Fox gave Pig a little box today.

Pig opened the little box.
Hip hip hooray!
Fox gave Pig a watch today!

Name _____

About the Play

Fill in the circle next to the correct answer.

1. Whose birthday is it?

   Ⓐ It is Ox's birthday.
   Ⓑ It is Pig's birthday.
   Ⓒ It is Fox's birthday.

2. What does Ox have?

   Ⓐ Ox has a big box.
   Ⓑ Ox has a little box.
   Ⓒ Ox has a watch.

3. What is in the little box?

   Ⓐ A fox is in the little box.
   Ⓑ A clock is in the little box.
   Ⓒ A watch is in the little box.

4. Who opened the boxes?

   Ⓐ Pig opened the boxes.
   Ⓑ Ox opened the boxes.
   Ⓒ Fox opened the boxes.

Name _____

I Know the Words

Fill in the circle next to the correct answer.

1. You can put a little watch in a _____.

   Ⓐ clock   Ⓑ fox   Ⓒ little box

2. You can tell time with a _____.

   Ⓐ box   Ⓑ watch   Ⓒ bed

3. You say "happy birthday" to a _____.

   Ⓐ clock   Ⓑ watch   Ⓒ friend

4. You can put a big clock in a _____.

   Ⓐ big box   Ⓑ little box   Ⓒ fox

5. You can open a _____.

   Ⓐ friend   Ⓑ box   Ⓒ fox

Name _____

I Know What Happened

Cut out the pictures. Glue them in order to show what happened in the play.

1 glue
2 glue
3 glue
4 glue

The Ring

This play is about a hen who has lost her ring.

 **Characters**

Hen   Duck   Cow   Cat   Chorus

1 Build Background

Ask students if they have ever lost anything. Then ask them to think about all the places they looked for the lost items. Did they look under the bed? Did they look in the car? Have each student name the item he or she lost and tell where it was found.

2 Assign Parts

The reading parts for Hen, Duck, Cow, and Cat are similar. Each part has a combination of simple, repetitive sentences and is well suited to students reading on grade level. The reading parts for the chorus contain a repetitive sentence frame that ends with a different prepositional phrase each time. The choral readings are well suited to students reading on or below grade level.

3 Introduce Vocabulary

Dictionary: Point to each pictured word. Read the word aloud and have students echo you. Discuss word meaning as needed.

Words to Know: Point to each word. Read the word aloud and have students echo you. Explain phonetic structures that are unfamiliar. For the word **found**, for example, you might say, *The letters **ou** in the word **found** sound like /ow/.* You might also want to point out the different pronunciations of the letter **o** in the words **looked**, **lost**, **poor**, and **your**. Discuss word meaning as needed.

4 Preview the Script

Guide students in previewing the script. Have students look at the illustrations and make predictions about what will happen in the play. Then go through the script again, page by page, having students highlight their reading parts.

5 Practice the Script and Share the Play

Have students read the script aloud as a group several times. Model how to use intonation and expression to reflect end punctuation. After students are able to read the script fluently, have them read the play for an audience.

6 Conduct Follow-up Activities

Model the chant for students. Talk about its rhythm. Have students echo you as you sing the chant again. Then have students sing the chant as a group.

Distribute practice pages 24–26 and guide students in completing them.

Dictionary

 bed

 chair

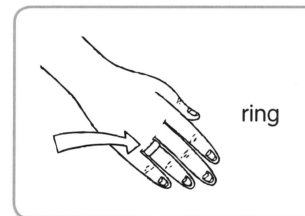 ring

 table

 under

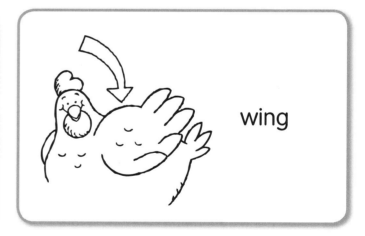 wing

Words to Know!

find	found	help	keep
looked	lost	poor	your

   Leveled Readers' Theater • EMC 3481 • © Evan-Moor Corp.

The Ring

Written by: Maya Jewel

_____
Name

Hen: Help! I lost my ring!

Duck: Did you look under the table?

Hen: Yes, I looked under the table.
My ring is not under the table.

Chorus: Poor Hen! Her ring is not under the table.

Duck: I will help you find your ring.
I will look on the table.

Hen: Is my ring on the table?

Duck: Your ring is not on the table.

Chorus: Poor Hen! Her ring is not on the table.

EMC 3481 • © Evan-Moor Corp.

Leveled Readers' Theater

Cow: Did you look under the chair?

Hen: Yes, I looked under the chair.
My ring is not under the chair.

Chorus: Poor Hen! Her ring is not under the chair.

EMC 3481 • © Evan-Moor Corp.

Leveled Readers' Theater

Cow: I will help you find your ring.
I will look on the chair.

Hen: Is my ring on the chair?

Cow: Your ring is not on the chair.

Chorus: Poor Hen! Her ring is not on the chair.

4

EMC 3481 • © Evan-Moor Corp.

Leveled Readers' Theater

Cat: I will help you find your ring.
I will look on the bed.

Hen: Is my ring on the bed?

Cat: Your ring is not on the bed.

Chorus: Poor Hen! Her ring is not on the bed.

5

Cat: Where do you keep your ring?

Chorus: Where does Hen keep her ring?

6

Hen: See my wing? This is where I keep my ring.

Cat: There it is! I see your ring!

Hen: Oh! My ring is on my wing!

Chorus: Hen found her ring.
Her ring was on her wing!

7

Sing to the tune of
"Here We Go 'Round the Mulberry Bush."

Lost and Found

Hen, poor Hen, has lost her ring,
    lost her ring, lost her ring.
Hen, poor Hen, has lost her ring.
Duck will help her find it.

Hen, poor Hen, has lost her ring,
    lost her ring, lost her ring.
Hen, poor Hen, has lost her ring.
Cow will help her find it.

Hen, poor Hen, has lost her ring,
    lost her ring, lost her ring.
Hen, poor Hen, has lost her ring.
Cat will help her find it.

Hen found her ring. It's on her wing,
    on her wing, on her wing.
Hen found her ring. It's on her wing.
That is where Cat found it.

Name _____

About the Play

Fill in the circle next to the correct answer.

1. Why did Hen need help?

   Ⓐ Hen lost her chair.
   Ⓑ Hen lost her table.
   Ⓒ Hen lost her ring.

2. Who helped Hen look first?

   Ⓐ Cat
   Ⓑ Duck
   Ⓒ Cow

3. Who helped Hen find her ring?

   Ⓐ Cat
   Ⓑ Duck
   Ⓒ Cow

4. Where was Hen's ring?

   Ⓐ on the table
   Ⓑ under the bed
   Ⓒ on her wing

Name _____

I Know the Words

Fill in the circle next to the correct answer.

1. You sleep in a _____.

   Ⓐ table   Ⓑ bed   Ⓒ chair

2. You eat at a _____.

   Ⓐ table   Ⓑ bed   Ⓒ chair

3. You sit in a _____.

   Ⓐ table   Ⓑ bed   Ⓒ chair

4. Your hand is where you find a _____.

   Ⓐ bed   Ⓑ ring   Ⓒ chair

5. You look for what you _____.

   Ⓐ lost   Ⓑ helped   Ⓒ found

Name _____

I Know What Happened

Cut out the pictures. Glue them in order of who helped Hen first, second, and third.

	① glue
	② glue
	③ glue

Leveled Readers' Theater • EMC 3481 • © Evan-Moor Corp.

A Pet for Jake

This play is about a boy who wants a pet.

Characters

Narrator   Jake   Clerk   Mom   Dad

---

1 Build Background

Discuss which animals make good pets and why they make good pets. Ask students questions such as *Would an elephant make a good pet? Why or why not?* Then invite each student to tell the class what kind of pet he or she has, using the following sentence frame: *I have a _____.*

2 Assign Parts

This play is well suited to students reading on grade level. All of the reading parts contain repetitive vocabulary and a few challenging words such as **quiet** and **sneeze.**

3 Introduce Vocabulary

Dictionary: Point to each pictured word. Read the word aloud and have students echo you. Discuss word meaning as needed.

Words to Know: Point to each word. Read the word aloud and have students echo you. Explain phonetic structures that are unfamiliar. For the word **quiet,** for example, you might say, *When you see the letters **qu** in a word, they sound like /kw/.* Discuss word meaning as needed.

4 Preview the Script

Guide students in previewing the script. Have students look at the illustrations and make predictions about what will happen in the play. Then go through the script again, page by page, having students highlight their reading parts.

5 Practice the Script and Share the Play

Have students read the script aloud as a group several times. Model how to use intonation and expression to reflect questions and statements. After students are able to read the script fluently, have them read the play for an audience.

6 Conduct Follow-up Activities

Model the chant for students. Talk about its rhythm and rhyme. Have students echo you as you sing the chant again. Then have students sing the chant as a group.

Distribute practice pages 34–36 and guide students in completing them.

Dictionary

 barks

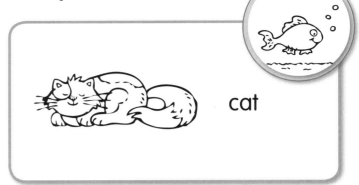 cat

 clerk

 dog

 fish

 fur

 pet shop

 sneeze

Words to Know!

good	idea	looked
makes	quiet	which

EMC 3481 • © Evan-Moor Corp.

A Pet for Jake

Written by: Annie Malls

Name _____

EMC 3481 • © Evan-Moor Corp.

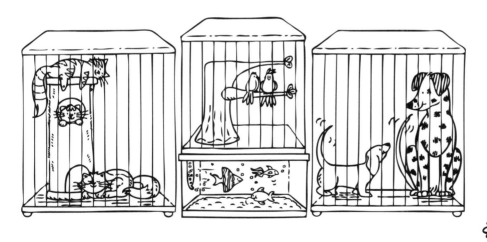

Narrator: Jake wants a pet.
He is at the pet shop.

Jake: Look at all the pets.
Which one can I get?

1

Clerk: May I help you?

Jake: I want a pet.

Clerk: A dog is a good pet.

Mom: A dog barks.

2

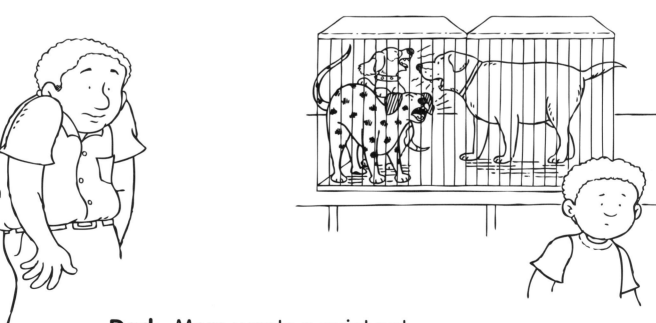

Dad: Mom wants a quiet pet.
A dog is not a quiet pet.

Jake: A dog is not a good pet for me to get.

3

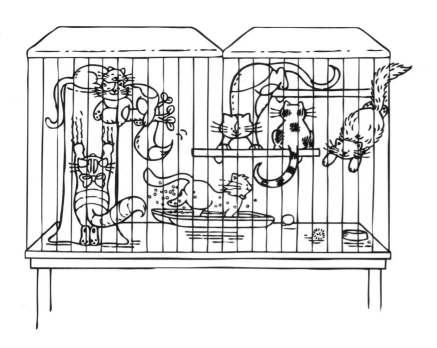

Clerk: A cat is a quiet pet.

Dad: A cat has fur.

4

Mom: The fur makes Dad sneeze.
Our pet should not make Dad sneeze.

Jake: A cat is not a good pet for me to get.

5

Narrator: The clerk looked at all the pets. Then she had an idea.

Clerk: A dog is not a good pet for you. A cat is not a good pet for you. Is a fish a good pet for you?

6

- -

Narrator: Jake looked at the fish.

Mom: A fish is quiet.

Dad: A fish will not make me sneeze.

Jake: Yes! A fish is a good pet for me to get!

7

Which Pet?

Jake wants to get a pet,
   get a pet, get a pet.
Jake wants to get a pet.
Which pet will Jake get?

Jake's mom wants a quiet pet,
   quiet pet, quiet pet.
Jake's mom wants a quiet pet.
Which pet will Jake get?

A fish would be a quiet pet,
   quiet pet, quiet pet.
A fish would be a quiet pet.
It's the pet that Jake will get.

Name _____

About the Play

Fill in the circle next to the correct answer.

1. What does Jake want?

   Ⓐ Jake wants a pen.
   Ⓑ Jake wants a pet.
   Ⓒ Jake wants a jet.

2. What kind of pet does Jake's mom want?

   Ⓐ Jake's mom wants a big pet.
   Ⓑ Jake's mom wants a pet that barks.
   Ⓒ Jake's mom wants a quiet pet.

3. What makes Jake's dad sneeze?

   Ⓐ Fur makes Jake's dad sneeze.
   Ⓑ Big pets make Jake's dad sneeze.
   Ⓒ Quiet pets make Jake's dad sneeze.

4. Which pet does Jake get?

   Ⓐ Jake gets a cat.
   Ⓑ Jake gets a dog.
   Ⓒ Jake gets a fish.

Name _____

I Know the Words

Fill in the circle next to the correct answer.

1. A pet shop _____.

   Ⓐ has pets   Ⓑ is quiet   Ⓒ does not have pets

2. Cats, dogs, and fish can all _____.

   Ⓐ have fins   Ⓑ be good pets   Ⓒ have fur

3. A dog is not a _____.

   Ⓐ quiet pet   Ⓑ big pet   Ⓒ pet

4. A cat _____.

   Ⓐ barks   Ⓑ has fur   Ⓒ has fins

5. Fur can make you _____.

   Ⓐ sneeze   Ⓑ swim   Ⓒ bark

Name _____

I Know What Happened

Cut out the pictures. Glue them in order of which pets Jake looked at first, second, and third.

① glue
② glue
③ glue

Leveled Readers' Theater • EMC 3481 • © Evan-Moor Corp.

Turtle and Frog

This play tells the story of a turtle and a frog who like to sit in the sun.

Narrator   Frog   Turtle   Chorus

1 **Build Background**

Discuss how the weather affects the temperature outside. Ask students what it feels like outside when the sun is shining. Then ask them what it feels like outside when clouds cover the sun. Explain to students that they will read a play about a turtle and a frog who like warm days. You might want to explain that turtles and frogs are animals that need the sun to keep warm.

2 **Assign Parts**

The reading parts for the narrator, Frog, and Turtle are well suited to students reading on grade level. The reading parts for the chorus are well suited to students reading on or below grade level.

3 **Introduce Vocabulary**

Dictionary: Point to each pictured word. Read the word aloud and have students echo you. Discuss word meaning as needed.

Words to Know: Point to each word. Read the word aloud and have students echo you. Explain phonetic structures that are unfamiliar. For the word **blew**, for example, you might say, *The letters ew in the word blew sound like /oo/.* Discuss word meaning as needed.

4 **Preview the Script**

Guide students in previewing the script. Have students look at the illustrations and make predictions about what will happen in the play. Then go through the script again, page by page, having students highlight their reading parts.

5 **Practice the Script and Share the Play**

Have students read the script aloud as a group several times. Model how to use intonation and expression to convey worry, ask a question, or make a statement. After students are able to read the script fluently, have them read the play for an audience.

6 **Conduct Follow-up Activities**

Model the chant for students. Talk about its rhythm and rhyme. Have students echo you as you sing the chant again. Then have students sing the chant as a group.

Distribute practice pages 44–46 and guide students in completing them.

Dictionary

cloud

frog

turtle

wind

Words to Know!

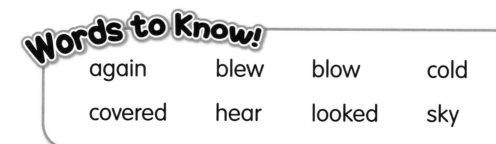

| again | blew | blow | cold |
| covered | hear | looked | sky |

EMC 3481 • © Evan-Moor Corp.

Turtle and Frog

Written by: Sonny Day

_____
Name

EMC 3481 • © Evan-Moor Corp.

Narrator: Turtle and Frog sat on a big rock.

Frog: Look at the sky!
The sun is out.
The day is warm.

Turtle: I like warm days.

Frog: I like to sit in the sun on warm days.

1

Narrator: Turtle looked up at the sky.

Turtle: What is that in the sky?

Frog: It is a cloud.

Turtle: I do not want a cloud in the sky today.

Chorus: Go away, cloud!

2

Frog: It is a big cloud.
It will cover the sun.

Turtle: Then we will be cold.
I do not like to be cold.

Chorus: Go away, cloud!

3

Narrator: The cloud covered the sun.

Turtle: I am cold!

Frog: So am I.

Chorus: Turtle and Frog are cold!

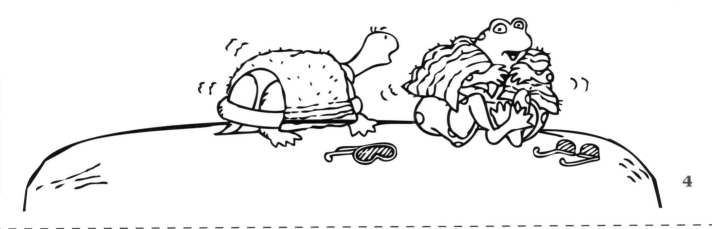

4

Turtle: What do I hear? Is that the wind?

Frog: Yes, it is the wind.

Turtle: I want the wind to blow the cloud away.

Chorus: Blow, wind, blow!

5

EMC 3481 • © Evan-Moor Corp.

Narrator: The wind blew the cloud away.

Frog: Look, the sun is out.

Turtle: I am warm.

Frog: So am I.

Chorus: Turtle and Frog are warm again!

6

EMC 3481 • © Evan-Moor Corp.

Turtle: I like warm days.

Frog: I like to sit in the sun.

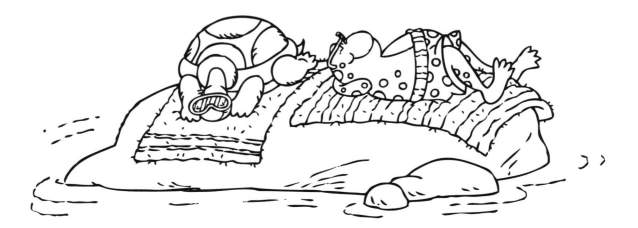

7

Blow, Blow, Blow

Blow, blow, blow the cloud
Way across the sky.
Merrily, merrily, merrily, merrily,
Good-bye, cloud, good-bye.

Blow, blow, blow the cloud
Away from the sun.
Merrily, merrily, merrily, merrily,
Then we'll have some fun!

Blow, blow, blow the cloud
Far, oh far, away.
Merrily, merrily, merrily, merrily,
It's a sunny day!

Name _____

About the Play

Fill in the circle next to the correct answer.

1. What does Turtle like?

   Ⓐ cold days
   Ⓑ warm days
   Ⓒ hot days

2. What does Frog like to do?

   Ⓐ sit under a cloud
   Ⓑ sit in the sun on warm days
   Ⓒ sit on his bed

3. What made Turtle and Frog cold?

   Ⓐ the wind blowing
   Ⓑ the sun
   Ⓒ a cloud covering the sun

4. What blew the clouds away from the sun?

   Ⓐ the rock
   Ⓑ the wind
   Ⓒ the clouds

Name _____

I Know the Words

Fill in the circle next to the correct answer.

1. The sun is in _____.

   Ⓐ a cloud   Ⓑ the sky   Ⓒ a rock

2. The sun makes you feel _____.

   Ⓐ cold   Ⓑ silly   Ⓒ warm

3. You can sit on _____.

   Ⓐ a rock   Ⓑ a cloud   Ⓒ water

4. You can hear _____.

   Ⓐ the sun   Ⓑ a rock   Ⓒ the wind

5. A cloud can cover _____.

   Ⓐ a rock   Ⓑ the sun   Ⓒ the wind

6. The wind can blow _____.

   Ⓐ a cloud   Ⓑ the sun   Ⓒ a rock

Name _____

Picture It

Follow the directions to draw the pictures.

1. Draw a turtle sitting in the sun.

2. Draw the sun and a cloud.

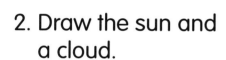

3. Draw what you like to do on a sunny day.

A Scary Sound

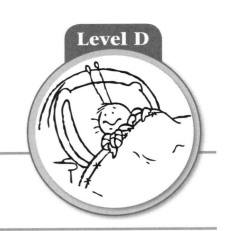

This play is about a bug that hears a scary sound.

Characters

Narrator   Noise   Bug   Rat   Chorus

1 Build Background

Ask students if they ever feel scared when they hear sounds they do not recognize. Explain that we sometimes feel scared when we hear, see, or feel something, and we do not know what it is. You might say, *I felt something touching my arm. I did not know what it was. I thought it might be a spider. I felt scared. But then I saw that it was just my cat's tail, and I was not scared anymore.* If time permits, ask students to tell the class about times when they felt scared.

2 Assign Parts

The reading parts for the narrator include challenging vocabulary words such as **blanket** and **window**, and are well suited to a student reading above grade level. The reading parts for Bug and Rat use repetitive vocabulary and are well suited to students reading on or above grade level. The reading parts for the noise and the chorus are short and repetitive and are well suited to students reading on or below grade level.

3 Introduce Vocabulary

Dictionary: Point to each pictured word. Read the word aloud and have students echo you. Discuss word meaning as needed.

Words to Know: Point to each word. Read the word aloud and have students echo you. Explain phonetic structures that are unfamiliar. For the word **sound**, for example, you might say, *The letters **ou** in the word **sound** sound like /ow/.* Discuss word meaning as needed.

4 Preview the Script

Guide students in previewing the script. Have students look at the illustrations and make predictions about what will happen in the play. Then go through the script again, page by page, having students highlight their reading parts.

5 Practice the Script and Share the Play

Have students read the script aloud as a group several times. Model how to use intonation and expression to convey fear. After students are able to read the script fluently, have them read the play for an audience.

6 Conduct Follow-up Activities

Model the chant for students. Talk about its rhythm. Have students echo you as you sing the chant again. Then have students sing the chant as a group.

Distribute practice pages 54–56 and guide students in completing them.

Dictionary

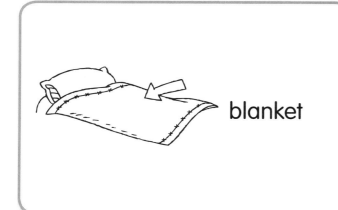
blanket

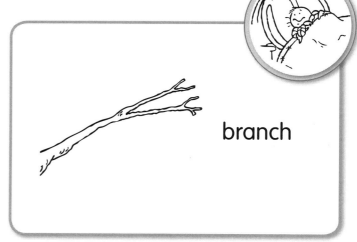
branch

called

scared

sleeping

window

Words to Know!

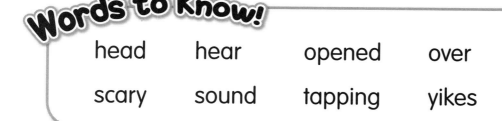

| head | hear | opened | over |
| scary | sound | tapping | yikes |

A Scary Sound

Written by: Bitsy Bug

_____
Name

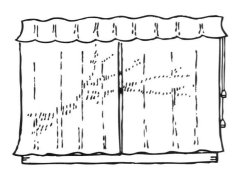

Narrator: Bug went to bed.

Noise: Tap, tap, tap!

Bug: Yikes! I hear a scary sound.

Chorus: What is that scary sound?

Narrator: Bug put the blanket over his head.

Noise: Tap, tap, tap!

Bug: I am scared. I cannot sleep.

Chorus: Bug is scared. He cannot sleep.

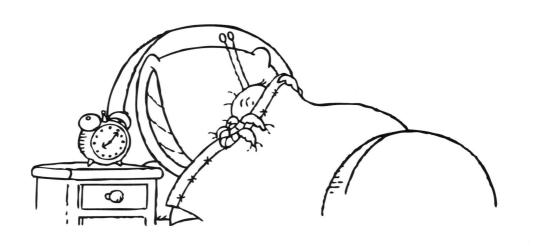

2

Narrator: Bug called Rat.

Bug: Hello, Rat. I am scared.
Will you come to my house?

Rat: Yes, I will come to your house.

3

Narrator: Bug ran back to bed.
He put the blanket over his head.

Noise: Rap, rap, rap!

Bug: Yikes! I hear a scary sound!

Chorus: What is that scary sound?

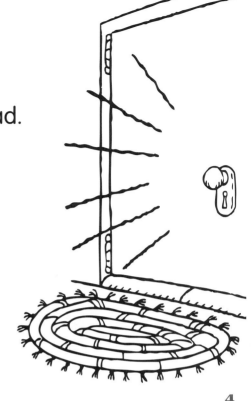

4

Noise: Rap, rap, rap!

Rat: Let me in, Bug. It is me, Rat.

Bug: Oh, it is Rat!

Narrator: Bug opened the door.

5

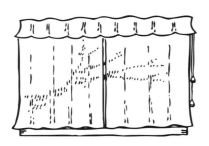

Noise: Tap, tap, tap!

Bug: Yikes! Did you hear that, Rat?

Chorus: Did Rat hear that?

Rat: It is at your window!

Narrator: Rat went to the window.

6

Rat: A branch is tapping at your window.

Bug: Oh, a branch is tapping.
I am not scared now.

Narrator: Bug went to bed.

Chorus: Shh. Bug is sleeping.

7

S-C-A-R-Y

There was a bug who heard a sound.
The sound was very scary.
S-c-a-r-y, s-c-a-r-y, s-c-a-r-y,
The sound was very scary.

It was a branch that made the sound.
The sound was very scary.
S-c-a-r-y, s-c-a-r-y, s-c-a-r-y,
The sound was very scary.

Tap, tap, tap, tap went the sound.
The sound was very scary.
S-c-a-r-y, s-c-a-r-y, s-c-a-r-y,
The sound was very scary.

Rat saw the branch that made the sound.
The sound was not so scary.
S-c-a-r-y, s-c-a-r-y, s-c-a-r-y,
The sound was not so scary.

Name _____

About the Play

Fill in the circle next to the correct answer.

1. What did Bug hear?

   Ⓐ Bug heard a funny sound.
   Ⓑ Bug heard a happy sound.
   Ⓒ Bug heard a scary sound.

2. Why did Bug call Rat?

   Ⓐ Bug was scared.
   Ⓑ Bug was happy.
   Ⓒ Bug was sleeping.

3. Where was the scary sound?

   Ⓐ The scary sound was on the blanket.
   Ⓑ The scary sound was at the window.
   Ⓒ The scary sound was in Bug's bed.

4. What made the scary sound?

   Ⓐ Bug made the scary sound.
   Ⓑ The blanket made the scary sound.
   Ⓒ A branch made the scary sound.

   Leveled Readers' Theater • EMC 3481 • © Evan-Moor Corp.

Name _____

I Know the Words

Fill in the circle next to the correct answer.

1. A branch is on a _____.

   Ⓐ bed   Ⓑ tree   Ⓒ window

2. You sleep _____.

   Ⓐ in a bed   Ⓑ on a branch   Ⓒ under a window

3. You can look out a _____.

   Ⓐ bed   Ⓑ branch   Ⓒ window

4. The cover on your bed is a _____.

   Ⓐ blanket   Ⓑ branch   Ⓒ door

5. You can open a _____.

   Ⓐ blanket   Ⓑ branch   Ⓒ door

Name _____

I Know What Happened

Cut out the pictures. Glue them in order to show what happened in the play.

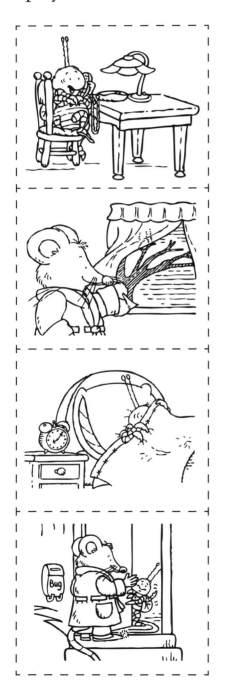

① glue
② glue
③ glue
④ glue

The Loose Tooth

This play is about a boy who has a loose tooth.

Narrator   Max   Clara   Emma   Marco

---

1 Build Background

Ask students to tell what it was like when they had a loose tooth. Model how to give an opinion on the best way to make a loose tooth come out. For example, you might say, *I think the best way to make a loose tooth come out is to jump up and down until the tooth falls out.* Then ask students to give their opinions on the best way to make a loose tooth come out.

2 Assign Parts

All of the reading parts in this play are well suited to students reading on or above grade level.

3 Introduce Vocabulary

Dictionary: Point to each pictured word. Read the word aloud and have students echo you. Discuss word meaning as needed.

Words to Know: Point to each word. Read the word aloud and have students echo you. Explain that a contraction is a shorter word made from two longer words. Point out that the apostrophe in a contraction shows where one or more letters are left out. Tell students that the word **doesn't** is the contraction for **does not**. Point out that the apostrophe in **doesn't** shows that a letter has been left out. Discuss word meaning as needed.

4 Preview the Script

Guide students in previewing the script. Have students look at the illustrations and make predictions about what will happen in the play. Then go through the script again, page by page, having students highlight their reading parts.

5 Practice the Script and Share the Play

Have students read the script aloud as a group several times. Model how to use intonation and expression to reflect end punctuation. After students are able to read the script fluently, have them read the play for an audience.

6 Conduct Follow-up Activities

Model the chant for students. Talk about its rhythm and rhyme. Have students echo you as you sing the chant again. Then have students sing the chant as a group.

Distribute practice pages 64–66 and guide students in completing them.

Dictionary

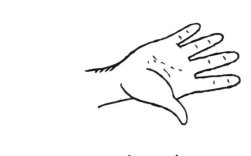

hand

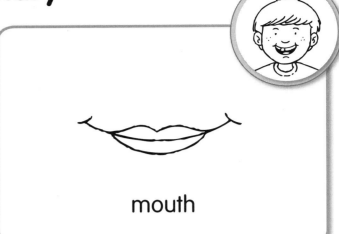

mouth

school

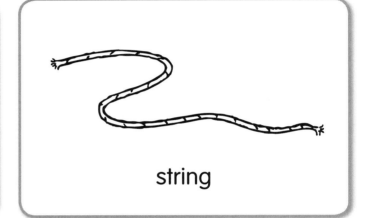

string

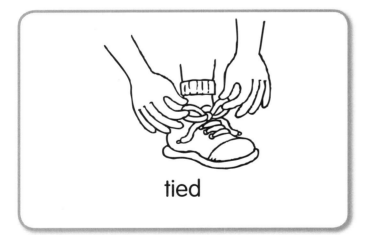

tied

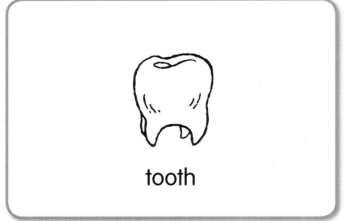

tooth

Words to Know!

brother	doesn't	flew	guess
loose	opened	scared	wiggled

Leveled Readers' Theater • EMC 3481 • © Evan-Moor Corp.

The Loose Tooth

Written by: Kenya Wigglet

_____
Name

Narrator: Max saw Clara on the way to school.

Max: Guess what, Clara? My tooth is loose!

Clara: Can I see?

Narrator: Max opened his mouth and wiggled his tooth.

Clara: Yep. Your tooth is loose.

1

Narrator: Max and Clara saw Emma.

Clara: Guess what, Emma? Max has a loose tooth.

Emma: Can I see?

2

Narrator: Max wiggled his tooth for Emma.

Emma: Yep. You have a loose tooth.

Max: It feels like it is going to come out.

3

Emma: My brother pulled out my loose tooth.
He tied a string around it.
He pulled the string, and the tooth came out.
I can pull out your tooth.

Max: No! I don't want my tooth to come out!

4

Narrator: Clara saw Marco.

Clara: Guess what, Marco? Max has a loose tooth.
But he doesn't want it to come out.

Marco: Why not, Max?

Max: It will hurt!

5

Marco: It will not—BOO!

Narrator: Marco scared Max.
Max's hand flew up and hit his tooth.

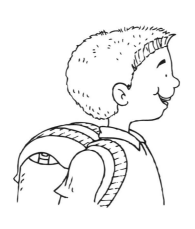

Max: My tooth came out!

Marco: Yep. And it didn't hurt, did it?

Can I See?

Oh what, oh what, does Max
   have in his mouth?
Oh what, oh what, can it be?

It's hard, and he wiggles it
   with his tongue.
His tooth must be loose!
Can I see?

Oh what, oh what, happened
   to Max's tooth?
Oh where, oh where, can it be?

It fell on the ground, but soon
   it was found.
His loose tooth came out!
Can I see?

Name _____

About the Play

Fill in the circle next to the correct answer.

1. Who has a loose tooth?

   Ⓐ Emma
   Ⓑ Clara
   Ⓒ Max

2. What does Emma want to do?

   Ⓐ tie a string around Max's loose tooth
   Ⓑ hit Max's loose tooth
   Ⓒ wiggle Max's loose tooth

3. Why doesn't Max want his tooth to come out?

   Ⓐ He has only one tooth.
   Ⓑ He thinks it will hurt.
   Ⓒ His tooth is not loose.

4. Who scared Max?

   Ⓐ Clara
   Ⓑ Emma
   Ⓒ Marco

Name _____

I Know the Words

Fill in the circle next to the correct answer.

1. You can wiggle _____.

   Ⓐ a car   Ⓑ a school   Ⓒ a loose tooth

2. You can open _____.

   Ⓐ a tooth   Ⓑ a string   Ⓒ your mouth

3. A loose tooth can be _____.

   Ⓐ pulled out   Ⓑ opened   Ⓒ scared

4. You can tie a _____.

   Ⓐ wiggle   Ⓑ string   Ⓒ mouth

5. If your brother says "boo!" you might be _____.

   Ⓐ tied   Ⓑ wiggled   Ⓒ scared

Name _____

I Know What Happened

Look at each picture. Write sentences to tell what happened in the play.

1. _____

_____

_____

_____

_____

2. _____

_____

_____

_____

_____

3. _____

_____

_____

_____

_____

Looking for a Party

This play is about children who make a game out of finding a friend's party.

Characters

Narrator   Noah   Matt   Sophia   Lee

---

1 Build Background

Tell students that this is a play about a party. Talk about all the different locations where a party might take place. For example, you might say, *You can have a party at a park.* Invite students to name places where they have been for parties. Then have students talk about what they like to do at parties and what they like to eat at parties.

2 Assign Parts

This play includes content vocabulary words such as **bedroom**, **kitchen**, and **backyard**. The reading parts for the narrator are well suited to students reading on or above grade level. The reading parts for Noah, Matt, Sophia, and Lee are well suited to students reading on grade level.

3 Introduce Vocabulary

Dictionary: Point to each pictured word. Read the word aloud and have students echo you. Explain phonetic structures that are unfamiliar. For the word **kitchen**, for example, you might say, *In the word **kitchen**, the letters **tch** sound like /ch/.* Discuss word meaning as needed.

Words to Know: Point to each word. Read the word aloud and have students echo you. Discuss word meaning as needed.

4 Preview the Script

Guide students in previewing the script. Have students look at the illustrations and make predictions about what will happen in the play. Then go through the script again, page by page, having students highlight their reading parts.

5 Practice the Script and Share the Play

Have students read the script aloud as a group several times. Model how to use intonation and expression to reflect end punctuation. After students are able to read the script fluently, have them read the play for an audience.

6 Conduct Follow-up Activities

Model the chant for students. Talk about its rhythm and rhyme. Have students echo you as you recite the chant again. Then have students recite the chant as a group.

Distribute practice pages 74–76 and guide students in completing them.

Dictionary

 bedroom

 cake

 hat

 ice cream

 kitchen

 living room

 party

 pizza

Words to Know!

asked	backyard	found	friends	looking
maybe	picked	show	start	surprise

Leveled Readers' Theater • EMC 3481 • © Evan-Moor Corp.

EMC 3481 • © Evan-Moor Corp.

Leveled Readers' Theater

Looking for a Party

Written by: Bill Loon

_____
Name

EMC 3481 • © Evan-Moor Corp.

Narrator: Noah asked his friends to come over.
Matt, Sophia, and Lee came over.

Noah: I have a surprise for you.

Matt: What is it?

Noah: You have to look for it.

Leveled Readers' Theater

Sophia: What are we looking for?

Noah: You are looking for a party!

Lee: A party! What fun!

Noah: Pick a card out of the hat.

2

Narrator: Matt picked a card.

Matt: My card has pizza on it.

Narrator: Then Sophia and Lee picked.

Sophia: I picked cake.

Lee: I picked ice cream. Now what?

3

Noah: Now you have to find the party!
The cards show what to look for.

Matt: Let's start looking!

Narrator: Matt ran into the living room.
Sophia ran into the bedroom.
Lee ran into the kitchen.

4

Matt: The party is not in the living room.

Noah: Keep looking!

Sophia: The party is not in the bedroom.

Noah: Keep looking!

5

Lee: The party is not in the kitchen.

Noah: Keep looking!

Sophia: Maybe the party is not in the house.

Narrator: Sophia ran to look in the backyard.

6

Sophia: I found it! I see the cake!

Lee: I see the ice cream!

Matt: I see the pizza!

Noah: Now we can have the party!

7

Find the Party

Find the pizza.
Find the cake.
Find the party.
Let's celebrate!

Look for hats and big balloons.
Look for yummy ice cream, too.
This is a party just for you!

You found the pizza
And the cake.
You found the party.
Let's celebrate!

Name _____

About the Play

Fill in the circle next to the correct answer.

1. What were Lee, Matt, and Sophia looking for?

   Ⓐ a ball
   Ⓑ a party
   Ⓒ a book

2. Who asked his friends to find the party?

   Ⓐ Noah
   Ⓑ Bill
   Ⓒ Matt

3. What did the cards show?

   Ⓐ animals
   Ⓑ books
   Ⓒ food

4. Where did Noah's friends find the party?

   Ⓐ in the kitchen
   Ⓑ in the backyard
   Ⓒ in the living room

Name _____

I Know the Words

Fill in the circle next to the correct answer.

1. It is fun to get a _____.

   Ⓐ surprise   Ⓑ kitchen   Ⓒ living room

2. At a party, you eat _____.

   Ⓐ a hat   Ⓑ cake   Ⓒ a card

3. You cook in a _____.

   Ⓐ bedroom   Ⓑ kitchen   Ⓒ living room

4. You sleep in a _____.

   Ⓐ bedroom   Ⓑ kitchen   Ⓒ living room

5. It is fun to go to a _____.

   Ⓐ party   Ⓑ bedroom   Ⓒ kitchen

Name _____

Picture It

Follow the directions to draw the pictures.

1. Draw a cake.

2. Draw an ice-cream cone.

3. Draw a pizza.

The Biggest!

This play is about three children who plant seeds in their backyard garden.

Level E

Characters

Narrator   May   Dad   Ken   Sue   Mom

---

1 Build Background

Explain to students that they are going to read a story about children who are growing a garden in their backyard. Talk about what a plant needs in order to grow. Ask students to raise their hands if they have ever planted something. Invite students to tell what kinds of plants they grew.

2 Assign Parts

The narrator has minimal reading parts that are well suited to students reading on grade level. The reading parts for May, Ken, and Sue are also well suited to students reading on grade level. The reading parts for Dad and Mom include content vocabulary and are well suited to students reading on or above grade level.

3 Introduce Vocabulary

Dictionary: Point to each pictured word. Read the word aloud and have students echo you. Discuss word meaning as needed.

Words to Know: Point to each word. Read the word aloud and have students echo you. Explain phonetic structures that are unfamiliar. For the word **might**, for example, you could say, *In the word **might**, the letters **ight** sound like /īt/.* Discuss word meaning as needed.

4 Preview the Script

Guide students in previewing the script. Have students look at the illustrations and make predictions about what will happen in the play. Then go through the script again, page by page, having students highlight their reading parts.

5 Practice the Script and Share the Play

Have students read the script aloud as a group several times. Model how to use intonation and expression to reflect end punctuation. After students are able to read the script fluently, have them read the play for an audience.

6 Conduct Follow-up Activities

Model the chant for students. Talk about its rhythm. Have students echo you as you sing the chant again. Then have students sing the chant as a group.

Distribute practice pages 84–86 and guide students in completing them.

Dictionary

 flowers

 garden

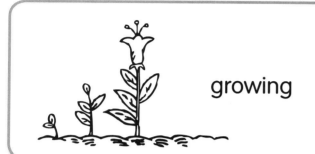 growing

 holes

 plant

 pumpkins

 seeds

 tomatoes

Words to Know!

about	children	going	might
passed	planting	should	water

The Biggest!

Written by: G. Arden

_____
Name

Narrator: May, Sue, and Ken are planting a garden.
Their mom and dad are helping them.

May: I want to plant flowers, Dad.
Big flowers! What should I do?

Dad: Dig some holes in the dirt.
Put flower seeds in the holes.
Then water the seeds every day.

1

Ken: I want to plant tomatoes, Dad.
Big tomatoes! What should I do?

Dad: Dig some holes in the dirt.
Put tomato seeds in the holes.
Then water the seeds every day.

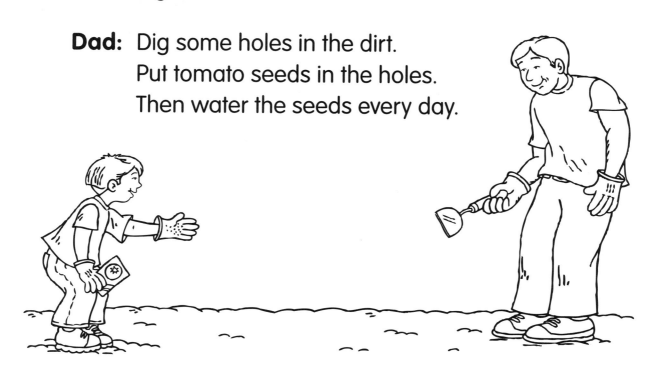

2

Sue: I want to plant pumpkins, Mom.
Big pumpkins! What should I do?

Mom: Dig some holes in the dirt.
Put pumpkin seeds in the holes.
Then water the seeds every day.

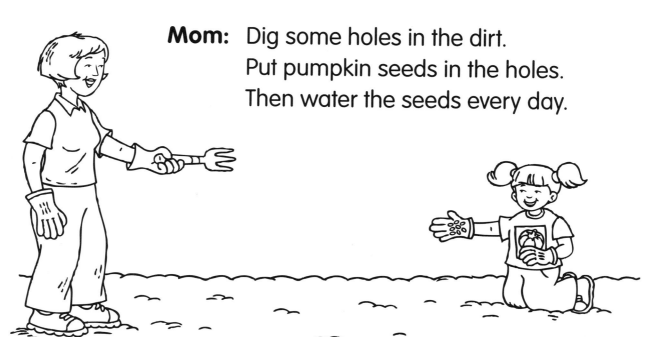

3

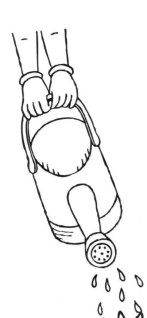

Narrator: Weeks passed. The children watered their seeds every day.

Mom: The garden is growing well.
May has a flower.
Sue has a pumpkin.
Ken has tomatoes.

4

Sue: My pumpkin is very big.

Ken: My tomatoes are big, too.
They are going to be bigger than pumpkins!

Dad: Tomatoes bigger than pumpkins?
We'll have to see about that.

5

EMC 3481 • © Evan-Moor Corp.

May: My flowers are going to be bigger than tomatoes and pumpkins!

Mom: Your flowers might be bigger than tomatoes, but bigger than pumpkins? We'll have to see about that.

6

EMC 3481 • © Evan-Moor Corp.

Narrator: More weeks passed.

Ken: Look at my tomato. It is big!

Sue: Look at my pumpkin! It is bigger!

May: Look at my flower! It is the biggest!

7

Who Planted the Garden?

Who planted the garden?
Who planted the garden?
Oh, oh, do you know
Who planted the garden?

May planted the flowers.
May planted the flowers.
Oh, oh, do you know
May planted the flowers?

Ken planted tomatoes.
Ken planted tomatoes.
Oh, oh, do you know
Ken planted tomatoes?

Sue planted pumpkins.
Sue planted pumpkins.
Oh, oh, do you know
Sue planted pumpkins?

Name _____

About the Play

Fill in the circle next to the correct answer.

1. You can dig holes in _____.

   Ⓐ dirt
   Ⓑ water
   Ⓒ seeds

2. Who planted pumpkin seeds?

   Ⓐ May
   Ⓑ Ken
   Ⓒ Sue

3. How long did it take the seeds to grow into plants?

   Ⓐ one day
   Ⓑ one week
   Ⓒ many weeks

4. Seeds will grow into plants if you _____.

   Ⓐ look at them
   Ⓑ water them
   Ⓒ sit next to them

     Leveled Readers' Theater • EMC 3481 • © Evan-Moor Corp.

Name _____

I Know the Words

Fill in the circle next to the correct answer.

1. You can dig _____.

    Ⓐ seeds   Ⓑ holes   Ⓒ tomatoes

2. A garden can have _____.

    Ⓐ flowers   Ⓑ a hat   Ⓒ a pet

3. You can eat _____.

    Ⓐ holes   Ⓑ dirt   Ⓒ tomatoes

4. You can plant _____.

    Ⓐ water   Ⓑ seeds   Ⓒ holes

5. A plant that is bigger than all the other plants is _____.

    Ⓐ the smallest   Ⓑ the newest   Ⓒ the biggest

Name _____

Picture It

Follow the directions to draw the pictures.

1. Draw a tomato plant.

2. Draw 5 seeds.

3. Draw a pumpkin.

Silly Kitty

This play is about a girl who has a playful pet cat.

Level F

Narrator   Sara   Grandma   Chorus

---

1. **Build Background**

   Ask students to raise their hands if they have a pet cat. Then have students use the sentence frames below to tell the cat's name and something silly the cat does.
   My cat's name is _____.
   My cat is silly because _____.

2. **Assign Parts**

   All of the reading parts in this play use rhyme. The narrator's parts are well suited to a student reading on grade level. The reading parts for Sara and Grandma are also well suited to students reading on grade level. The reading parts for the chorus are well suited to students reading below grade level.

3. **Introduce Vocabulary**

   Dictionary: Point to each pictured word. Read the word aloud and have students echo you. Explain phonetic structures that are unfamiliar. For the words **treat** and **meat**, for example, you might say, *The letters ea in the words treat and meat sound like /ē/.* Discuss word meaning as needed.

   Words to Know: Point to each word. Read the word aloud and have students echo you. Discuss word meaning as needed.

4. **Preview the Script**

   Guide students in previewing the script. Have students look at the illustrations and make predictions about what will happen in the play. Then go through the script again, page by page, having students highlight their reading parts.

5. **Practice the Script and Share the Play**

   Have students read the script aloud as a group several times. Model how to use intonation and expression to emphasize the rhyme. After students are able to read the script fluently, have them read the play for an audience.

6. **Conduct Follow-up Activities**

   Model the chant for students. Talk about its rhythm and rhyme. Have students echo you as you recite the chant again. Then have students recite the chant as a group.

   Distribute practice pages 94–96 and guide students in completing them.

Dictionary

 dinner

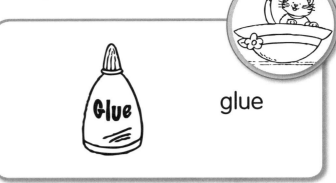 glue

 hair

 head

 meat

 picture

 Silly Kitty

 treat

Words to Know!

cannot	come	does	done
making	ready	tummy	yummy

Leveled Readers' Theater • EMC 3481 • © Evan-Moor Corp.

EMC 3481 • © Evan-Moor Corp.

Leveled Readers' Theater

Silly Kitty

Written by: Ivana Palay

_____
Name

EMC 3481 • © Evan-Moor Corp.

Leveled Readers' Theater

Narrator: Sara is making a picture today.
But her kitty cat wants her to play.

Sara: Silly Kitty, go away.
I am making a picture.
I cannot play.

Chorus: Go away, Silly Kitty!

1

Narrator: The kitty is playing with Sara's hair.
Sara does not want him there.

Sara: Silly Kitty, go to bed.
Your toy is there, not on my head.

Chorus: Go to bed, Silly Kitty!

2

Sara: Silly Kitty wants to play.
But I am busy.
He is in my way.

Grandma: Dinner is ready. Come and eat.
I will give the cat a treat.

3

Narrator: Sara ate her corn and meat.
Her cat ate up his kitty treat.

Sara: Thank you, Grandma. Dinner was yummy!
And Kitty says "thanks" for filling his tummy.
Where is Silly Kitty?

4

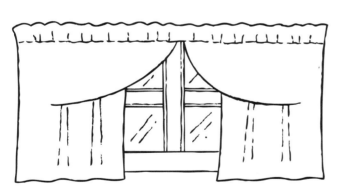

Grandma: I see the cat. He is in my hat!
Jump down from there.
That is not your mat!

Chorus: Jump down now, Silly Kitty!

5

Sara: Soon my picture will be done.
Be a good kitty. Then we'll have fun.

Chorus: Be good, Silly Kitty!

6

Sara: Come and look, Grandma.
My picture is done. It looks so pretty.
And it was fun.

Grandma: I see your kitty had fun, too.
Look at his fur. It is full of glue.

Chorus: Look at Silly Kitty!

7

Chant

Follow the rhythm and rhyme to recite
this chant.

Silly Kitty!

Silly Kitty wants to play.
Silly Kitty, go away!
Silly Kitty, sit on your mat.
Silly Kitty, that's my hat!

Silly Kitty wants to play.
Silly Kitty, go away!
Silly Kitty, sit on your bed.
Silly Kitty, that's my head!

Silly Kitty wants to play.
Silly Kitty, go away!
Silly Kitty, now what did you do?
Silly Kitty, I love you!

Name _____

About the Play

Fill in the circle next to the correct answer.

1. What was Sara making?

   Ⓐ dinner
   Ⓑ a picture
   Ⓒ a cat toy

2. What did Silly Kitty want to do?

   Ⓐ play
   Ⓑ eat
   Ⓒ sleep

3. What did Sara eat?

   Ⓐ a kitty treat
   Ⓑ a picture
   Ⓒ corn and meat

4. Silly Kitty liked to _____.

   Ⓐ sleep a lot
   Ⓑ play a lot
   Ⓒ jump a lot

Name _____

I Know the Words

Fill in the circle next to the correct answer.

1. You can make _____.

    Ⓐ hair   Ⓑ glue   Ⓒ a picture

2. You can eat _____.

    Ⓐ glue   Ⓑ dinner   Ⓒ a hat

3. You sit on a _____.

    Ⓐ mat   Ⓑ hat   Ⓒ treat

4. You sleep in a _____.

    Ⓐ picture   Ⓑ hat   Ⓒ bed

5. You eat to fill your _____.

    Ⓐ tummy   Ⓑ bed   Ⓒ picture

Name _____

I Know What Happened

Cut out the pictures. Glue them in order to show what happened in the play.

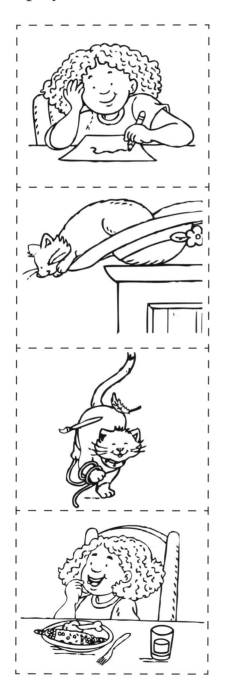

① **glue**
② **glue**
③ **glue**
④ **glue**

The Ant and the Dove

This play tells the story of an ant and a dove that are true friends.

Characters

Narrator   Ant   Dove   Man   Chorus

1 Build Background
Discuss what it means to be a friend. Ask each student to say a word that tells how a friend acts or what a friend does. Then ask students if they can think of a time when they helped a friend, and have a few students share their stories.

2 Assign Parts
The narrator has the most frequent and lengthy reading parts. This role is well suited to a student reading above grade level. The reading parts for Ant, Dove, and the man are well suited to students reading on grade level. The reading parts for the chorus are somewhat repetitive and are well suited to students reading on or below grade level.

3 Introduce Vocabulary
Dictionary: Point to each pictured word. Read the word aloud and have students echo you. Discuss word meaning as needed.

Words to Know: Point to each word. Read the word aloud and have students echo you. Explain phonetic structures that are unfamiliar. For the word **heard**, for example, you might say, *In the word **heard**, the letters **ear** sound like /ur/.* Discuss word meaning as needed.

4 Preview the Script
Guide students in previewing the script. Have students look at the illustrations and make predictions about what will happen in the play. Then go through the script again, page by page, having students highlight their reading parts.

5 Practice the Script and Share the Play
Have students read the script aloud as a group several times. Model how to use intonation and expression to convey distress, fear, or pain. After students are able to read the script fluently, have them read the play for an audience.

6 Conduct Follow-up Activities
Model the chant for students. Talk about its rhythm. Have students echo you as you recite the chant again. Then have students recite the chant as a group.

Distribute practice pages 104–106 and guide students in completing them.

Dictionary

 drink

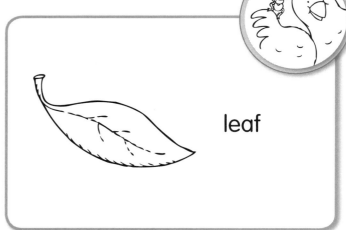 leaf

 net

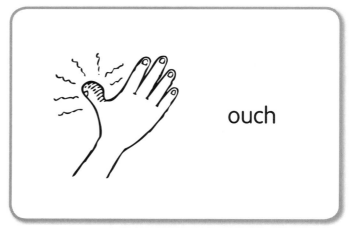 ouch

 river

 swim

Words to Know!

fell	flew	friend	grab
heard	helping	safe	yelled

Leveled Readers' Theater • EMC 3481 • © Evan-Moor Corp.

EMC 3481 • © Evan-Moor Corp.

Leveled Readers' Theater

The Ant and the Dove

Written by: Bess Friends

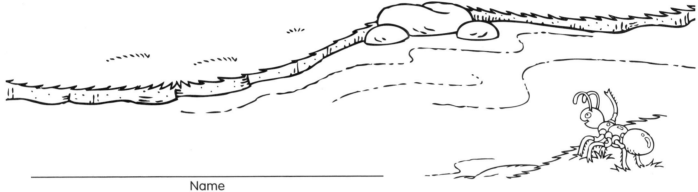

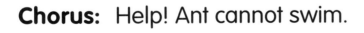

Name

EMC 3481 • © Evan-Moor Corp.

Narrator: One day, Ant went to the river to drink water. She fell into the water. She yelled for help.

Ant: Help! I cannot swim!

Chorus: Help! Ant cannot swim.

Leveled Readers' Theater

1

Dove: I will help you, Ant!

Narrator: Dove put a leaf into the water.

Dove: Grab the leaf, Ant!

Chorus: Grab the leaf, Ant!

2

Narrator: Ant grabbed the leaf and held on. Ant was safe.

Ant: Thank you for helping me, Dove. I am happy that you are my friend.

Chorus: Dove and Ant are friends. Friends help each other.

3

Narrator: The next day, Ant saw a man with a net.

Man: I have a net.
I am going to get that dove.

Chorus: Help! The man has a net.
He is going to get Dove!

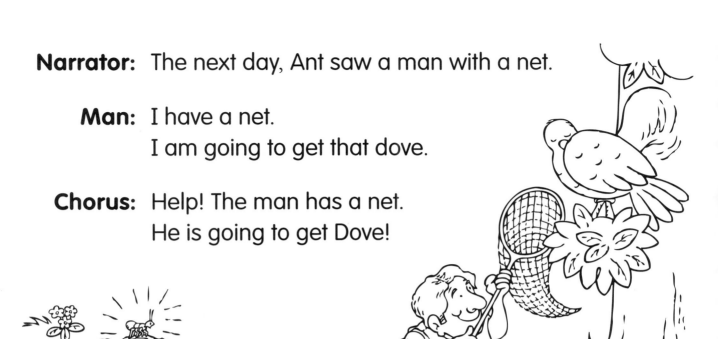

4

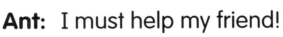

Ant: I must help my friend!
I know how to help Dove!

Narrator: Ant ran up the man's leg.
Then Ant bit the man's leg.

Man: Ouch! Ouch!
An ant bit my leg.

Chorus: Ouch! Ant bit the man's leg!

5

Narrator: The man yelled.
Dove heard the man yell.
Dove saw the man with the net.

Ant: Fly, Dove! Fly away!

6

Narrator: Dove flew away.
Soon the man went away.
Then Dove came back.

Dove: Thank you for helping me, Ant!
I am happy that you are my friend.

Chorus: Ant and Dove are friends.
Friends help each other.

7

Friends

Friends play together,
  together, together.
Friends play together.
That's what friends do.

Friends share stories,
  stories, stories.
Friends share stories.
That's what friends do.

Friends help each other,
  each other, each other.
Friends help each other.
That's what friends do.

Name _____

About the Play

Fill in the circle next to the correct answer.

1. How did Dove help Ant?

   Ⓐ Dove put a leaf into the water.
   Ⓑ Dove jumped into the water.
   Ⓒ Dove gave Ant a net.

2. What did the man have?

   Ⓐ The man had a leaf.
   Ⓑ The man had Dove.
   Ⓒ The man had a net.

3. How did Ant save Dove?

   Ⓐ Ant gave Dove a leaf.
   Ⓑ Ant gave the man a net.
   Ⓒ Ant bit the man's leg.

4. Why did Ant and Dove help each other?

   Ⓐ They wanted to swim.
   Ⓑ They are friends.
   Ⓒ They were in a net.

     Leveled Readers' Theater • EMC 3481 • © Evan-Moor Corp.

Name _____

I Know the Words

Fill in the circle next to the correct answer.

1. You can swim _____.

   Ⓐ in a net   Ⓑ in water   Ⓒ on a leaf

2. You stand on your _____.

   Ⓐ leg   Ⓑ leaf   Ⓒ fly

3. You can catch a dove with _____.

   Ⓐ water   Ⓑ a net   Ⓒ a leaf

4. You say "ouch" when you _____.

   Ⓐ fly   Ⓑ swim   Ⓒ get hurt

5. To **grab** means to _____.

   Ⓐ hold onto   Ⓑ fly   Ⓒ drink

Name _____

I Know What Happened

Cut out the pictures. Glue them in order to show what happened in the play.

① glue
② glue
③ glue
④ glue

   Leveled Readers' Theater • EMC 3481 • © Evan-Moor Corp.

Fun All Year

This play is about children who have fun as the seasons change.

Characters

Carlos   Felipe   Lisa   Jordan

---

1 Build Background

Discuss the current season. Model how to use describing words to talk about the season and the weather. For example, you might say, *It is summer. It is warm and sunny outside.* Then ask students if they can think of any other words that describe the season.

2 Assign Parts

This play includes content vocabulary words such as **winter** and **snow**. All of the reading parts are well suited to students reading on or above grade level.

3 Introduce Vocabulary

Dictionary: Point to each pictured word. Read the word aloud and have students echo you. Explain phonetic structures that are unfamiliar. For the word **leaves**, for example, you might say, *The letters **ea** in the word **leaves** sound like /ēē/.* Discuss word meaning as needed.

Words to Know: Point to each word. Read the word aloud and have students echo you. Point out that **fall** is a multiple-meaning word. Discuss word meaning as needed.

4 Preview the Script

Guide students in previewing the script. Have students look at the illustrations and make predictions about what will happen in the play. Then go through the script again, page by page, having students highlight their reading parts.

5 Practice the Script and Share the Play

Have students read the script aloud as a group several times. Model how to use intonation and expression to convey excitement. After students are able to read the script fluently, have them read the play for an audience.

6 Conduct Follow-up Activities

Model the chant for students. Talk about its rhythm. Have students echo you as you sing the chant again. Then have students sing the chant as a group.

Distribute practice pages 116–118 and guide students in completing them.

Dictionary

 baby birds

 horse

 leaves

 nest

 snow

 water

Words to Know!

fall	falling	feels	gone	making
pile	ride	spring	summer	winter

EMC 3481 • © Evan-Moor Corp.

Fun All Year

Written by: Rollin N. Snow

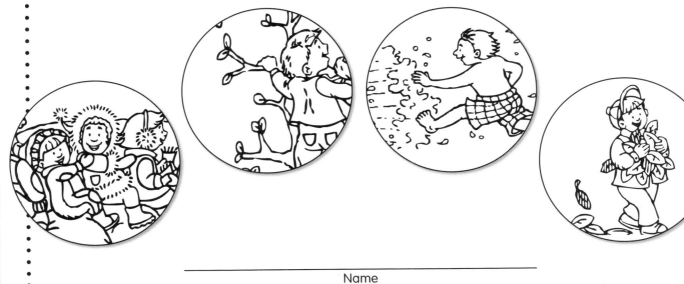

_____

Name

EMC 3481 • © Evan-Moor Corp.

Carlos: Winter is here!
Look at the snow on the tree.
All of the leaves are gone.

Felipe: Let's go out and play.
I see Lisa and Jordan.

1

Lisa: We are making a snow horse.

Carlos: Can I ride the snow horse?

Felipe: I want to ride the snow horse, too!

Jordan: We can all ride the snow horse.

Lisa: Winter is fun!

2

Carlos: Spring is here!
Look at the leaves on the tree.
They are new and little.

Felipe: Let's go out and play.
I see Lisa and Jordan.

3

Jordan: I see a nest in the tree.

Lisa: Are there baby birds in the nest?

Carlos: I will go up the tree and see!

Felipe: I want to see, too!

4

Carlos: I see three eggs in the nest.

Felipe: I want to see the eggs, too!

Jordan: Let's all go up and see the eggs! Spring is fun!

5

EMC 3481 • © Evan-Moor Corp.

Carlos: Summer is here!
Look at the leaves on the tree.
They are big and green.

Felipe: Let's go out and play.
I see Lisa and Jordan.

6

EMC 3481 • © Evan-Moor Corp.

Jordan: It is hot today.
I am playing in the water.

Felipe: I want to play in the water, too!

Jordan: We can all play in the water.

Lisa: Water feels good on a hot day.
Summer is fun!

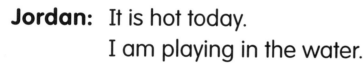

7

EMC 3481 • © Evan-Moor Corp.

Carlos: Fall is here!
Look at the leaves on the tree.
They are yellow and red.
And they are falling!

Felipe: Let's go out and play.
I see Lisa and Jordan.

8

EMC 3481 • © Evan-Moor Corp.

Lisa: I want to play in the leaves.

Jordan: Let's make a pile of leaves!

Carlos: I will help make a pile of leaves.

Felipe: I want to help, too.

Jordan: We can all help make a pile of leaves.

9

Lisa: I want to jump in the leaves.

Felipe: I want to jump in the leaves, too.

Jordan: We can all jump in the leaves.

Lisa: Jumping in the leaves is fun.
Fall is fun!

10

Carlos: Look! I see snow.
Let's go out and play.
Let's find Lisa and Jordan.

Felipe: We have fun with Lisa and Jordan.
We have fun all year!

11

Four Seasons

In winter, in winter,
We see snow. We see snow.
We can make a snow horse.
We can make a snow horse.
Winter's fun. Winter's fun.

In spring, in spring,
Leaves are new. Leaves are new.
Birds lay eggs in nests.
Birds lay eggs in nests.
Spring is fun. Spring is fun.

In summer, in summer,
It is hot. It is hot.
We play in the water.
We play in the water.
Summer's fun. Summer's fun.

In fall, in fall,
Trees lose leaves. Trees lose leaves.
We jump in the piles.
We jump in the piles.
Fall is fun. Fall is fun.

Name _____

About the Play

Fill in the circle next to the correct answer.

1. What can you do in winter?

   Ⓐ play in the water
   Ⓑ play in the snow
   Ⓒ look at eggs in a nest

2. What can you do in spring?

   Ⓐ play in the leaves
   Ⓑ play in the snow
   Ⓒ look at eggs in a nest

3. What can you do in summer?

   Ⓐ play in the water
   Ⓑ play in the snow
   Ⓒ look at eggs in a nest

4. What can you do in fall?

   Ⓐ play in the leaves
   Ⓑ play in the snow
   Ⓒ look at eggs in a nest

                                    Leveled Readers' Theater • EMC 3481 • © Evan-Moor Corp.

Name _____

I Know the Words

Fill in the circle next to the correct answer.

1. Snow falls in _____.

   Ⓐ summer   Ⓑ winter   Ⓒ fall

2. Baby birds are born in _____.

   Ⓐ fall   Ⓑ spring   Ⓒ winter

3. Leaves fall off a _____.

   Ⓐ tree   Ⓑ horse   Ⓒ nest

4. You can see baby birds in _____.

   Ⓐ water   Ⓑ a nest   Ⓒ snow

5. You can ride _____.

   Ⓐ a bird   Ⓑ a horse   Ⓒ an egg

6. You can play in the _____.

   Ⓐ birds   Ⓑ eggs   Ⓒ water

Name _____

Picture It

Follow the directions to draw the pictures.

1. Draw a tree with snow on it.

2. Draw a tree that has a lot of leaves.

3. Draw a bird's nest in a tree.

The Boy Who Yelled Wolf

This play is a retelling of the folk tale The Boy Who Cried Wolf.
It is about a boy who does not tell the truth.

Characters

Narrator   Father   Boy   Farmers

---

1 Build Background

Explain to students that they will read a story about a boy who does not tell the truth. Then discuss what it means to tell the truth. Invite students to share reasons why it is important to tell the truth.

2 Assign Parts

All of the reading parts in this play are well suited to students reading on or above grade level. The narrator has the most frequent reading parts. The farmers' parts are read chorally.

3 Introduce Vocabulary

Dictionary: Point to each pictured word. Read the word aloud and have students echo you. Discuss word meaning as needed.

Words to Know: Point to each word. Read the word aloud and have students echo you. Explain phonetic structures that are unfamiliar. For the word **enough**, for example, you might say, *In the word **enough**, the letters **ough** sound like /uff/.* Discuss word meaning as needed.

4 Preview the Script

Guide students in previewing the script. Have students look at the illustrations and make predictions about what will happen in the play. Then go through the script again, page by page, having students highlight their reading parts.

5 Practice the Script and Share the Play

Have students read the script aloud as a group several times. Model how to use intonation and expression to reflect end punctuation. After students are able to read the script fluently, have them read the play for an audience.

6 Conduct Follow-up Activities

Model the chant for students. Talk about its rhythm and rhyme. Have students echo you as you recite the chant again. Then have students recite the chant as a group.

Distribute practice pages 128–130 and guide students in completing them.

Dictionary

 farmers

 hear

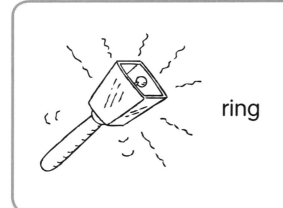 ring

 scare

 sheep

 yell

Words to Know!

alone	enough	having	trick
turned	walked	watch	wolf

EMC 3481 • © Evan-Moor Corp.

The Boy Who Yelled Wolf

A retelling of *The Boy Who Cried Wolf*

_____

Name

EMC 3481 • © Evan-Moor Corp.

Narrator: A boy and his father had many sheep. The father was happy when the boy turned ten years old.

Father: Now you are old enough to watch the sheep. You can take them to the hill to eat grass. You must take them every day.

1

Narrator: The father gave the boy a bell.

Father: Ring this bell if you see a wolf. Then yell for help. The farmers will run up the hill. They will scare the wolf away.

Narrator: Day after day, the sheep ate grass on the hill. Day after day, the boy watched the sheep.

Boy: The sheep just eat grass all day. I want to have some fun. I will play a trick on the farmers. I will ring the bell. Then I will yell.

Narrator: The boy rang the bell.

Boy: Help! A wolf! Help! Help!

Farmers: We hear a bell. We hear the boy on the hill.
He is yelling. We must help him.

4

Narrator: The farmers ran up the hill.

Farmers: We are here to help you.
Where is the wolf? We will not
let the wolf get your sheep.

5

Boy: There is no wolf. I was just having some fun.

Farmers: You must not ring the bell or yell if you do not need help.

6

Narrator: The farmers went back down the hill. Many more days passed.

Boy: I never see a wolf. I want to have some fun. I will ring my bell and yell. It will make the farmers run.

7

Farmers: We hear a bell! The boy is yelling for help!

Narrator: The farmers ran up the hill. They looked around. They did not see a wolf.

Farmers: Where is the wolf?

Boy: There is no wolf. I just wanted to have some fun.

Farmers: You must not ring the bell or yell if you do not need help.

Narrator: The next day, the boy saw a wolf.
He rang the bell. He yelled and yelled.

Boy: Help! A wolf! Help! Help!

Narrator: The farmers did not come.
The wolf scared the sheep away.
The boy walked down the hill alone.

10

Boy: Father, a wolf scared the sheep away!
I rang the bell. I yelled for help.
The farmers did not come!

Father: You played tricks on the farmers.
You wanted to have fun. The farmers
like to have fun, too. This time, the
farmers tricked you!

11

Ring the Bell and Yell

The boy will ring the bell.
He will ring the bell and yell.
There is no wolf, but—shh—don't tell.
The boy will ring the bell and yell.

The farmers hear the bell.
They hear the bell and yell.
"Where's the wolf? We hear the bell.
If there's no wolf, you should not yell!"

He did not ring the bell.
He did not ring or yell.
The farmers said, "You have done well.
You did not ring the bell or yell."

Name _____

About the Play

Fill in the circle next to the correct answer.

1. Who had to watch the sheep?

   Ⓐ the farmers
   Ⓑ the wolf
   Ⓒ the boy

2. What happened the first time the boy rang the bell and yelled?

   Ⓐ The farmers came to help.
   Ⓑ A wolf ate the sheep.
   Ⓒ No one came to help.

3. What happened the last time the boy rang the bell and yelled?

   Ⓐ The farmers came to help.
   Ⓑ A wolf ate the sheep.
   Ⓒ No one came to help.

4. Who tricked the boy?

   Ⓐ the farmers
   Ⓑ his father
   Ⓒ the sheep

Name _____

I Know the Words

Fill in the circle next to the correct answer.

1. Sheep eat _____.

    Ⓐ grass   Ⓑ bells   Ⓒ farmers

2. You ring a _____.

    Ⓐ boy   Ⓑ wolf   Ⓒ bell

3. If you need help, you _____.

    Ⓐ eat   Ⓑ yell   Ⓒ play a trick

4. You hear a bell _____.

    Ⓐ yell   Ⓑ play a trick   Ⓒ ring

5. You run up a _____.

    Ⓐ hill   Ⓑ ring   Ⓒ sheep

Name _____

I Know What Happened

Cut out the pictures. Glue them in order to show what happened in the play.

① glue
② glue
③ glue
④ glue

   Leveled Readers' Theater • EMC 3481 • © Evan-Moor Corp.

Woods Walk

This informational play is about a family that goes on a guided walk through the woods.

Characters

Guide   Mom   Lena   Trent

1 Build Background

Ask students if they have ever walked through woods or a forest. Talk about the characteristics of a forest environment. Then have students brainstorm names of animals that live in woods, and post their responses.

2 Assign Parts

The reading parts for the guide include content vocabulary words such as **ground** and **cave** and are well suited to students reading above grade level. The reading parts for Mom, Lena, and Trent also contain a few content vocabulary words, but the parts are short in length, so they are well suited to students reading on grade level.

3 Introduce Vocabulary

Dictionary: Point to each pictured word. Read the word aloud and have students echo you. Discuss word meaning as needed.

Words to Know: Point to each word. Read the word aloud and have students echo you. Explain phonetic structures that are unfamiliar. For the word **ground**, for example, you might say, *The letters **ou** in the word **ground** sound like /ow/.* Discuss word meaning as needed.

4 Preview the Script

Guide students in previewing the script. Have students look at the illustrations and make predictions about what will happen in the play. Then go through the script again, page by page, having students highlight their reading parts.

5 Practice the Script and Share the Play

Have students read the script aloud as a group several times. Model how to use intonation and expression to convey excitement or fear. After students are able to read the script fluently, have them read the play for an audience.

6 Conduct Follow-up Activities

Model the chant for students. Talk about its rhythm. Have students echo you as you sing the chant again. Then have students sing the chant as a group.

Distribute practice pages 140–142 and guide students in completing them.

Dictionary

 animals

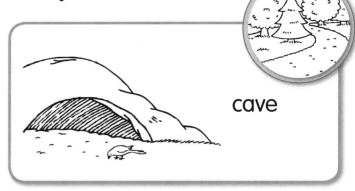 cave

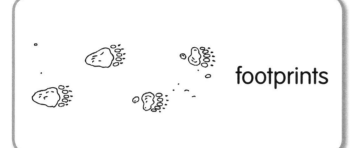 footprints

 nest

 robin

 squirrels

 wolf

 woods

Words to Know!

ground	jumped	live	night	ready
safe	sounds	under	walk	wild

Leveled Readers' Theater • EMC 3481 • © Evan-Moor Corp.

EMC 3481 • © Evan-Moor Corp.

Leveled Readers' Theater

Woods Walk

Written by: Forest Walker

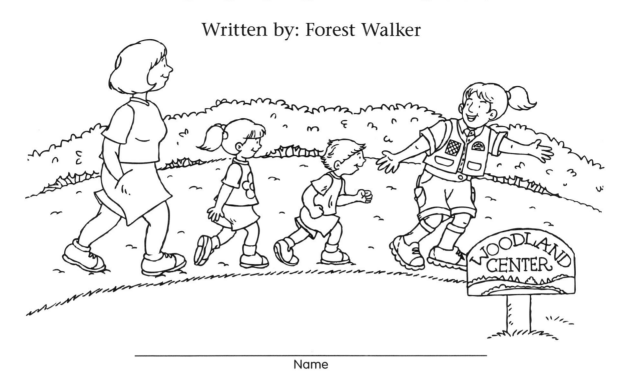

_____
Name

EMC 3481 • © Evan-Moor Corp.

Leveled Readers' Theater

Guide: Hi, Lena. Hi, Trent. I'm happy that you and your mom are here today. Are you ready for our Woods Walk?

Mom: Will we see wild animals? Will we be safe?

Guide: We will see how animals live in the wild, but the Woods Walk is safe.

Lena: Look! I see a robin!

Trent: I can see robins at home.
I want to see a wolf.

Mom: Oh no! Not a wolf!

Guide: You won't see a wolf in these woods.

2

Mom: I see some squirrels, kids.
Do you see them up there in the tree?

Trent: I wish I lived in a tree.

3

Lena: I see a big nest!

Trent: Hey! A squirrel jumped out of it!

Guide: It's a squirrel's nest.

4

Mom: Do many animals make nests in trees?

Guide: Yes, and some animals make nests in the ground. These ants have a nest in the ground.

Lena: Look, Mom. I can see the ants' nest.

5

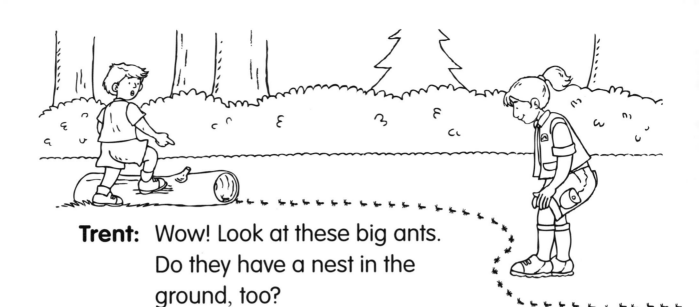

Trent: Wow! Look at these big ants. Do they have a nest in the ground, too?

Guide: No, these big ants make their nests in wood. They live in the log that's under your foot.

Mom: Oh my! Trent, get off that log!

Lena: Mom! I think I see a fox.

Mom: A fox? No, there can't be a fox here!

Lena: It is a fox! I can tell by its tail.

Trent: Where does the fox live?

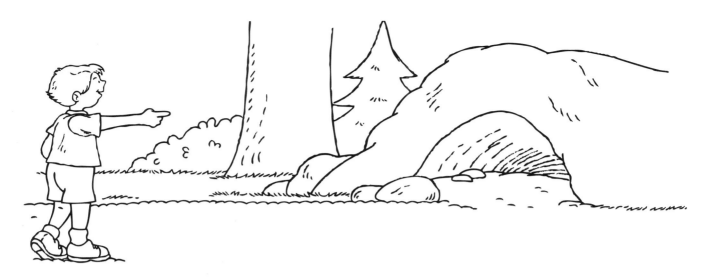

Guide: It lives in a den. Some foxes make dens in the ground. Others make dens in trees or logs. And some foxes even live in caves.

Trent: There's a cave! Can we go in it?

8

Guide: That's a bear's cave, Trent. Do you see the footprints?

Lena: Don't bears go in caves when it's cold?

Guide: Yes. When it's cold, bears sleep in caves.

Mom: It feels a little cold right now. I think we'd better go home!

9

Guide: Don't worry, our Woods Walk is over now.

Lena: I wish we could see more animals.

Guide: Many of the animals that live here only come out at night.

10

Trent: Then I want to take a Woods Walk at night!

Mom: A night walk? In the woods? In the dark?

Guide: We don't have a night walk, Trent. But, next week, we're having a Wildflower Walk.

Mom: A Wildflower Walk sounds nice and safe!

11

Walking in the Woods

Walking in the woods.
Walking in the woods.
A robin! A robin!
In a nest.

Walking in the woods.
Walking in the woods.
A squirrel! A squirrel!
Up a tree.

Walking in the woods.
Walking in the woods.
Some ants! Some ants!
Under a log.

Walking in the woods.
Walking in the woods.
A fox! A fox!
In a den.

Walking in the woods.
Walking in the woods.
A bear! A bear!
By a cave.

Name _____

About the Play

Fill in the circle next to the correct answer.

1. Where was the family walking?

   Ⓐ in the house
   Ⓑ in the woods
   Ⓒ in the hills

2. Which animal was in a nest?

   Ⓐ a bear
   Ⓑ a squirrel
   Ⓒ a fox

3. What animal left footprints outside a cave?

   Ⓐ a bear
   Ⓑ a squirrel
   Ⓒ a fox

4. What kind of walks does Mom like?

   Ⓐ walks that are scary
   Ⓑ walks that are safe
   Ⓒ walks that are long

    Leveled Readers' Theater • EMC 3481 • © Evan-Moor Corp.

Name _____

I Know the Words

Fill in the circle next to the correct answer.

1. A squirrel is _____.

   Ⓐ an animal   Ⓑ a log   Ⓒ a flower

2. A den is _____.

   Ⓐ an animal   Ⓑ a log   Ⓒ an animal's home

3. A fox makes a _____.

   Ⓐ flower   Ⓑ den   Ⓒ nest

4. A bear's den may be _____.

   Ⓐ in a cave   Ⓑ in a nest   Ⓒ in a log

5. You can walk in _____.

   Ⓐ woods   Ⓑ nests   Ⓒ logs

Name _____

Picture It

Follow the directions to draw the pictures.

1. Draw an animal that lives in a den.

2. Draw an animal that lives in a nest.

3. Draw an animal and its footprints.

Jackie and the Beanstalk

This play is a retelling of the fairy tale Jack and the Beanstalk.

Characters

Storyteller	Mother	Jackie	Man
Woman	Giant		

1 Build Background
Discuss the difference between real and make-believe. Explain that many stories are make-believe. Tell students that another word for **make-believe** is **fiction**. Remind students of fictional stories that they have recently read or heard.

2 Assign Parts
Most of the reading parts in this play are well suited to students reading above grade level. Many of the reading parts contain long vowel words, diphthongs, and short and long vowel digraphs.

3 Introduce Vocabulary
Dictionary: Point to each pictured word. Read the word aloud and have students echo you. Explain phonetic structures that are unfamiliar. For the word **soup**, for example, you might say, *The letters **ou** in the word **soup** sound like* /ōō/, *as in* **tool**. Discuss word meaning as needed.

Words to Know: Point to each word. Read the word aloud and have students echo you. Point out the silent **b** in **climb**. Discuss word meaning as needed.

4 Preview the Script
Guide students in previewing the script. Have students look at the illustrations and make predictions about what will happen in the play. Then go through the script again, page by page, having students highlight their reading parts.

5 Practice the Script and Share the Play
Have students read the script aloud as a group several times. Model how to use intonation and expression to convey sadness, anger, worry, or excitement. After students are able to read the script fluently, have them read the play for an audience.

6 Conduct Follow-up Activities
Model the chant for students. Talk about its rhythm. Have students echo you as you sing the chant again. Then have students sing the chant as a group.

Distribute practice pages 152–154 and guide students in completing them.

Dictionary

 beans

 beanstalk

 chopped

 hide

 money

 soup

 tossed

 window

Words to Know!

| buy | climb | clouds | giant | mother |
| once | quick | rich | safe | upon |

Leveled Readers' Theater • EMC 3481 • © Evan-Moor Corp.

Jackie
and the
Beanstalk

A retelling of *Jack and the Beanstalk*

_____
Name

Storyteller: Once upon a time, a girl named Jackie lived with her mother in a little house. One day, they ran out of food.

Mother: We need food, Jackie. But I do not have any money. We will have to sell our cow.

1

Leveled Readers' Theater

Jackie: I will sell our cow for a lot of money.
Then we can buy food.

Storyteller: Jackie went to town to sell the cow.
She met a man on the road.

Man: I will give you these beans for your cow.

2

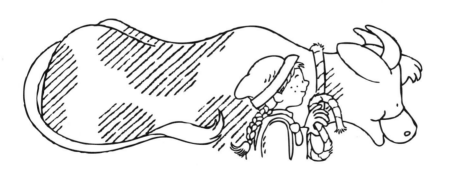

Jackie: I cannot sell my cow for beans!
I need money to buy food.

Man: These beans are better than money.
They will make you rich!

Storyteller: Jackie took the beans. She gave
the man the cow and ran home.

Leveled Readers' Theater

3

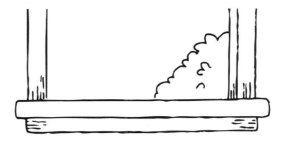

Jackie: Look, Mother! I sold our cow for these beans.
The man said they would make us rich!

Mother: We cannot buy food with beans!

Storyteller: Jackie's mother tossed the beans out the window.
The next day, she had a big surprise.

4

Mother: Eek! A giant beanstalk!

Jackie: Wow! Those beans grew fast!
I am going to climb the beanstalk.

Storyteller: Jackie climbed up, up, up.
She climbed past the clouds.
At the top, she saw a big house.

5

Jackie: That is a very big house!

Storyteller: Jackie ran up to the house.
A woman opened the door.

Woman: Go away, little girl! A giant lives here.
He eats children. Oh no! I hear the giant.
You must hide!

6

Giant: Yum! I smell a child.
Did you cook a child for my lunch?

Woman: No. I made soup for you to eat.

Giant: Soup again? Bring me my golden hen!

7

Storyteller: The woman gave the giant a golden cage.
The cage had a golden hen in it.

Giant: Lay an egg, Hen!

Storyteller: Jackie saw the hen lay a golden egg.
Then she saw the giant fall asleep.

8

Jackie: The giant is asleep. Now I can get out
of here. I will take the hen with me.

Storyteller: Jackie took the hen and ran.
But the giant woke up!

9

Giant: A child! Yum! Stop, child!

Storyteller: The giant ran after Jackie, but Jackie was too quick. She slid down, down, down the beanstalk. Then she chopped it down. Jackie was safe.

10

Jackie: Mother! Mother! Look at this hen. It lays golden eggs!

Mother: Hens do not lay golden eggs!

Storyteller: But the hen did lay golden eggs! Jackie and her mother were rich. And now, they had lots of food, too. Yum!

11

Who Is It?

Who's afraid of the hungry giant,
　the hungry giant, the hungry giant?
Who's afraid of the hungry giant?
Who, oh who, is it?

Who ran away with the golden cage,
　the golden cage, the golden cage?
Who ran away with the golden cage?
Who, oh who, is it?

Who chopped down the big beanstalk,
　the big beanstalk, the big beanstalk?
Who chopped down the big beanstalk?
Who, oh who, is it?

Who got rich with the golden eggs,
　the golden eggs, the golden eggs?
Who got rich with the golden eggs?
Who, oh who, is it?

Name _____

About the Play

Fill in the circle next to the correct answer.

1. Why did Jackie and her mother need money?

   Ⓐ to buy a cow
   Ⓑ to buy food
   Ⓒ to buy beans

2. Why did Jackie's mother toss the beans out the window?

   Ⓐ because Jackie did not sell the cow
   Ⓑ because Jackie sold the hen
   Ⓒ because Jackie's mother could not buy food with beans

3. What did the beans grow into?

   Ⓐ a giant beanstalk
   Ⓑ a giant bean
   Ⓒ a giant

4. What made Jackie and her mother rich?

   Ⓐ a cow that gave a lot of milk
   Ⓑ a giant beanstalk
   Ⓒ a hen that could lay golden eggs

Name _____

I Know the Words

Fill in the circle next to the correct answer.

1. Beans can grow into a _____.

   Ⓐ girl   Ⓑ beanstalk   Ⓒ giant

2. You can buy food with _____.

   Ⓐ beans   Ⓑ a hen   Ⓒ money

3. You eat _____.

   Ⓐ soup   Ⓑ money   Ⓒ a man

4. Clouds are in the _____.

   Ⓐ window   Ⓑ house   Ⓒ sky

5. If you did it one time, you did it _____.

   Ⓐ once   Ⓑ always   Ⓒ never

6. A giant is a very _____.

   Ⓐ big person   Ⓑ small person   Ⓒ tiny bird

Name _____

I Know What Happened

Cut out the pictures. Glue them in order to show what happened in the play.

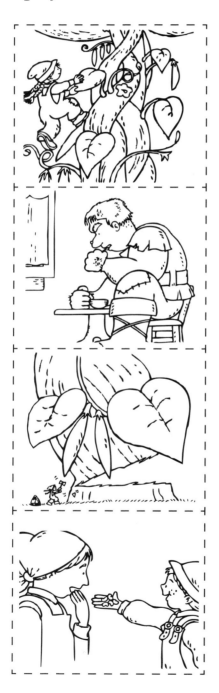

①   glue
②   glue
③   glue
④   glue

Answer Key

Page 14

Comprehension Activity

Name _____

About the Play

Fill in the circle next to the correct answer.

1. Whose birthday is it?
   - Ⓐ It is Ox's birthday.
   - ● It is Pig's birthday.
   - Ⓒ It is Fox's birthday.

2. What does Ox have?
   - ● Ox has a big box.
   - Ⓑ Ox has a little box.
   - Ⓒ Ox has a watch.

3. What is in the little box?
   - Ⓐ A fox is in the little box.
   - Ⓑ A clock is in the little box.
   - ● A watch is in the little box.

4. Who opened the boxes?
   - ● Pig opened the boxes.
   - Ⓑ Ox opened the boxes.
   - Ⓒ Fox opened the boxes.

14   Birthday Time

Page 15

Vocabulary Activity

Name _____

I Know the Words

Fill in the circle next to the correct answer.

1. You can put a little watch in a _____.
   - Ⓐ clock
   - Ⓑ fox
   - ● little box

2. You can tell time with a _____.
   - Ⓐ box
   - ● watch
   - Ⓒ bed

3. You say "happy birthday" to a _____.
   - Ⓐ clock
   - Ⓑ watch
   - ● friend

4. You can put a big clock in a _____.
   - ● big box
   - Ⓑ little box
   - Ⓒ fox

5. You can open a _____.
   - Ⓐ friend
   - ● box
   - Ⓒ fox

Birthday Time   15

Page 16

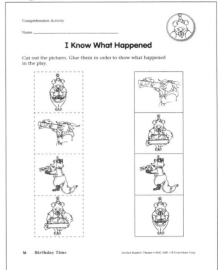

Comprehension Activity

Name _____

I Know What Happened

Cut out the pictures. Glue them in order to show what happened in the play.

16   Birthday Time

Page 24

Comprehension Activity

Name _____

About the Play

Fill in the circle next to the correct answer.

1. Why did Hen need help?
   - Ⓐ Hen lost her chair.
   - ● Hen lost her table.
   - ● Hen lost her ring.

2. Who helped Hen look first?
   - Ⓐ Cat
   - ● Duck
   - Ⓒ Cow

3. Who helped Hen find her ring?
   - ● Cat
   - Ⓑ Duck
   - Ⓒ Cow

4. Where was Hen's ring?
   - Ⓐ on the table
   - Ⓑ under the bed
   - ● on her wing

24   The Ring

Page 25

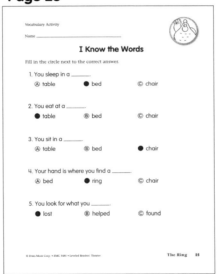

Vocabulary Activity

Name _____

I Know the Words

Fill in the circle next to the correct answer.

1. You sleep in a _____.
   - Ⓐ table
   - ● bed
   - Ⓒ chair

2. You eat at a _____.
   - ● table
   - Ⓑ bed
   - Ⓒ chair

3. You sit in a _____.
   - Ⓐ table
   - Ⓑ bed
   - ● chair

4. Your hand is where you find a _____.
   - Ⓐ bed
   - ● ring
   - Ⓒ chair

5. You look for what you _____.
   - ● lost
   - Ⓑ helped
   - Ⓒ found

The Ring   25

Page 26

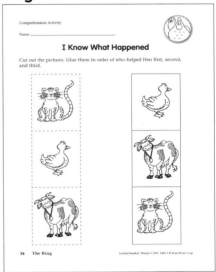

Comprehension Activity

Name _____

I Know What Happened

Cut out the pictures. Glue them in order of who helped Hen first, second, and third.

26   The Ring

Page 34

Comprehension Activity

Name _____

About the Play

Fill in the circle next to the correct answer.

1. What does Jake want?
   - Ⓐ Jake wants a pen.
   - ● Jake wants a pet.
   - Ⓒ Jake wants a jet.

2. What kind of pet does Jake's mom want?
   - Ⓐ Jake's mom wants a big pet.
   - Ⓑ Jake's mom wants a pet that barks.
   - ● Jake's mom wants a quiet pet.

3. What makes Jake's dad sneeze?
   - ● Fur makes Jake's dad sneeze.
   - Ⓑ Big pets make Jake's dad sneeze.
   - Ⓒ Quiet pets make Jake's dad sneeze.

4. Which pet does Jake get?
   - Ⓐ Jake gets a cat.
   - Ⓑ Jake gets a dog.
   - ● Jake gets a fish.

34   A Pet for Jake

Page 35

Vocabulary Activity

Name _____

I Know the Words

Fill in the circle next to the correct answer.

1. A pet shop _____.
   - ● has pets
   - Ⓑ is quiet
   - Ⓒ does not have pets

2. Cats, dogs, and fish can all _____.
   - Ⓐ have fins
   - ● be good pets
   - Ⓒ have fur

3. A dog is not a _____.
   - ● quiet pet
   - Ⓑ big pet
   - Ⓒ pet

4. A cat _____.
   - Ⓐ barks
   - ● has fur
   - Ⓒ has fins

5. Fur can make you _____.
   - ● sneeze
   - Ⓑ swim
   - Ⓒ bark

A Pet for Jake   35

Page 36

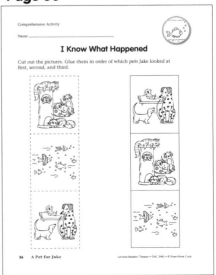

Comprehension Activity

Name _____

I Know What Happened

Cut out the pictures. Glue them in order of which pets Jake looked at first, second, and third.

36   A Pet for Jake

Page 44

Comprehension Activity

Name _____

About the Play

Fill in the circle next to the correct answer.

1. What does Turtle like?
   - Ⓐ cold days
   - ● warm days
   - Ⓒ hot days

2. What does Frog like to do?
   - Ⓐ sit under a cloud
   - ● sit in the sun on warm days
   - Ⓒ sit on his bed

3. What made Turtle and Frog cold?
   - Ⓐ the wind blowing
   - Ⓑ the sun
   - ● a cloud covering the sun

4. What blew the clouds away from the sun?
   - Ⓐ the rock
   - ● the wind
   - Ⓒ the clouds

44   Turtle and Frog

Page 45

Vocabulary Activity

Name _____

I Know the Words

Fill in the circle next to the correct answer.

1. The sun is in _____.
   - Ⓐ a cloud
   - ● the sky
   - Ⓒ a rock

2. The sun makes you feel _____.
   - Ⓐ cold
   - Ⓑ silly
   - ● warm

3. You can sit on _____.
   - ● a rock
   - Ⓑ a cloud
   - Ⓒ water

4. You can hear _____.
   - Ⓐ the sun
   - Ⓑ a rock
   - ● the wind

5. A cloud can cover _____.
   - Ⓐ a rock
   - ● the sun
   - Ⓒ the wind

6. The wind can blow _____.
   - ● a cloud
   - Ⓑ the sun
   - Ⓒ a rock

Turtle and Frog   45

Page 46

Comprehension Activity

Name _____

Picture It

Follow the directions to draw the pictures.

1. Draw a turtle sitting in the sun.

   Drawings will vary.

2. Draw the sun and a cloud.

3. Draw what you like to do on a sunny day.

46   Turtle and Frog

Page 54

Comprehension Activity

Name _____

About the Play

Fill in the circle next to the correct answer.

1. What did Bug hear?
   - Ⓐ Bug heard a funny sound.
   - Ⓑ Bug heard a happy sound.
   - ● Bug heard a scary sound.

2. Why did Bug call Rat?
   - ● Bug was scared.
   - Ⓑ Bug was happy.
   - Ⓒ Bug was sleeping.

3. Where was the scary sound?
   - Ⓐ The scary sound was on the blanket.
   - ● The scary sound was at the window.
   - Ⓒ The scary sound was in Bug's bed.

4. What made the scary sound?
   - Ⓐ Bug made the scary sound.
   - Ⓑ The blanket made the scary sound.
   - ● A branch made the scary sound.

54   A Scary Sound

Page 55

Vocabulary Activity

Name _____

I Know the Words

Fill in the circle next to the correct answer.

1. A branch is on a _____.
   - Ⓐ bed
   - ● tree
   - Ⓒ window

2. You sleep _____.
   - ● in a bed
   - Ⓑ on a branch
   - Ⓒ under a window

3. You can look out a _____.
   - Ⓐ bed
   - Ⓑ branch
   - ● window

4. The cover on your bed is a _____.
   - ● blanket
   - Ⓑ branch
   - Ⓒ door

5. You can open a _____.
   - Ⓐ blanket
   - Ⓑ branch
   - ● door

A Scary Sound   55

Page 56

Comprehension Activity

Name _____

I Know What Happened

Cut out the pictures. Glue them in order to show what happened in the play.

56   A Scary Sound

Page 64

Comprehension Activity

Name _____

About the Play

Fill in the circle next to the correct answer.

1. Who has a loose tooth?
   - Ⓐ Emma
   - Ⓑ Clara
   - ● Max

2. What does Emma want to do?
   - ● tie a string around Max's loose tooth
   - Ⓑ hit Max's loose tooth
   - Ⓒ wiggle Max's loose tooth

3. Why doesn't Max want his tooth to come out?
   - Ⓐ He has only one tooth.
   - ● He thinks it will hurt.
   - Ⓒ His tooth is not loose.

4. Who scared Max?
   - Ⓐ Clara
   - Ⓑ Emma
   - ● Marco

64   The Loose Tooth

Page 65

Vocabulary Activity

Name _____

I Know the Words

Fill in the circle next to the correct answer.

1. You can wiggle _____.
   - Ⓐ a car
   - Ⓑ a school
   - ● a loose tooth

2. You can open _____.
   - Ⓐ a tooth
   - Ⓑ a string
   - ● your mouth

3. A loose tooth can be _____.
   - ● pulled out
   - Ⓑ opened
   - Ⓒ scared

4. You can tie a _____.
   - Ⓐ wiggle
   - ● string
   - Ⓒ mouth

5. If your brother says "boo!" you might be _____.
   - Ⓐ tied
   - Ⓑ wiggled
   - ● scared

The Loose Tooth   65

Page 66

Comprehension Activity

Name _____

I Know What Happened

Look at each picture. Write sentences to tell what happened in the play.

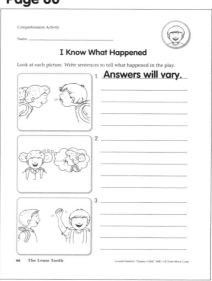

1. **Answers will vary.**
_____

2. _____

3. _____

66   The Loose Tooth

Page 74

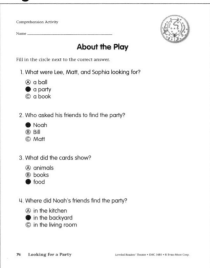

Comprehension Activity
Name _____

About the Play

Fill in the circle next to the correct answer.

1. What were Lee, Matt, and Sophia looking for?
   - Ⓐ a ball
   - ● a party
   - Ⓒ a book

2. Who asked his friends to find the party?
   - ● Noah
   - Ⓑ Bill
   - Ⓒ Matt

3. What did the cards show?
   - Ⓐ animals
   - Ⓑ books
   - ● food

4. Where did Noah's friends find the party?
   - Ⓐ in the kitchen
   - ● in the backyard
   - Ⓒ in the living room

74   Looking for a Party

Page 75

Vocabulary Activity
Name _____

I Know the Words

Fill in the circle next to the correct answer.

1. It is fun to get a _____.
   - ● surprise
   - Ⓑ kitchen
   - Ⓒ living room

2. At a party, you eat _____.
   - Ⓐ a hat
   - ● cake
   - Ⓒ a card

3. You cook in a _____.
   - Ⓐ bedroom
   - ● kitchen
   - Ⓒ living room

4. You sleep in a _____.
   - ● bedroom
   - Ⓑ kitchen
   - Ⓒ living room

5. It is fun to go to a _____.
   - ● party
   - Ⓑ bedroom
   - Ⓒ kitchen

Looking for a Party   75

Page 76

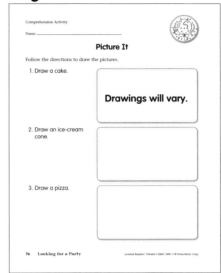

Comprehension Activity
Name _____

Picture It

Follow the directions to draw the pictures.

1. Draw a cake.

   Drawings will vary.

2. Draw an ice-cream cone.

3. Draw a pizza.

76   Looking for a Party

Page 84

Comprehension Activity
Name _____

About the Play

Fill in the circle next to the correct answer.

1. You can dig holes in _____.
   - ● dirt
   - Ⓑ water
   - Ⓒ seeds

2. Who planted pumpkin seeds?
   - Ⓐ May
   - Ⓑ Ken
   - ● Sue

3. How long did it take the seeds to grow into plants?
   - Ⓐ one day
   - Ⓑ one week
   - ● many weeks

4. Seeds will grow into plants if you _____.
   - Ⓐ look at them
   - ● water them
   - Ⓒ sit next to them

84   The Biggest!

Page 85

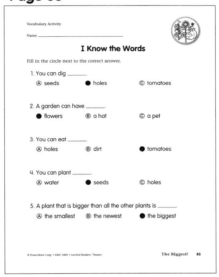

Vocabulary Activity
Name _____

I Know the Words

Fill in the circle next to the correct answer.

1. You can dig _____.
   - Ⓐ seeds
   - ● holes
   - Ⓒ tomatoes

2. A garden can have _____.
   - ● flowers
   - Ⓑ a hat
   - Ⓒ a pet

3. You can eat _____.
   - Ⓐ holes
   - Ⓑ dirt
   - ● tomatoes

4. You can plant _____.
   - Ⓐ water
   - ● seeds
   - Ⓒ holes

5. A plant that is bigger than all the other plants is _____.
   - Ⓐ the smallest
   - Ⓑ the newest
   - ● the biggest

The Biggest!   85

Page 86

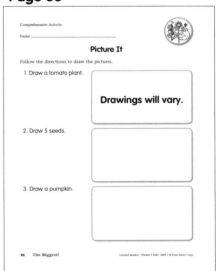

Comprehension Activity
Name _____

Picture It

Follow the directions to draw the pictures.

1. Draw a tomato plant.

   Drawings will vary.

2. Draw 5 seeds.

3. Draw a pumpkin.

86   The Biggest!

Page 94

Comprehension Activity
Name _____

About the Play

Fill in the circle next to the correct answer.

1. What was Sara making?
   - Ⓐ dinner
   - ● a picture
   - Ⓒ a cat toy

2. What did Silly Kitty want to do?
   - ● play
   - Ⓑ eat
   - Ⓒ sleep

3. What did Sara eat?
   - Ⓐ a kitty treat
   - Ⓑ a picture
   - ● corn and meat

4. Silly Kitty liked to _____.
   - Ⓐ sleep a lot
   - ● play a lot
   - Ⓒ jump a lot

94   Silly Kitty

Page 95

Vocabulary Activity
Name _____

I Know the Words

Fill in the circle next to the correct answer.

1. You can make _____.
   - Ⓐ hair
   - Ⓑ glue
   - ● a picture

2. You can eat _____.
   - Ⓐ glue
   - ● dinner
   - Ⓒ a hat

3. You sit on a _____.
   - ● mat
   - Ⓑ hat
   - Ⓒ treat

4. You sleep in a _____.
   - Ⓐ picture
   - Ⓑ hat
   - ● bed

5. You eat to fill your _____.
   - ● tummy
   - Ⓑ bed
   - Ⓒ picture

Silly Kitty   95

Page 96

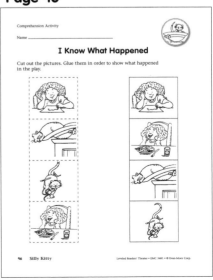

Comprehension Activity
Name _____

I Know What Happened

Cut out the pictures. Glue them in order to show what happened in the play.

96   Silly Kitty

Page 104

Comprehension Activity

Name _____

About the Play

Fill in the circle next to the correct answer.

1. How did Dove help Ant?
   - ● Dove put a leaf into the water.
   - Ⓑ Dove jumped into the water.
   - Ⓒ Dove gave Ant a net.

2. What did the man have?
   - Ⓐ The man had a leaf.
   - Ⓑ The man had Dove.
   - ● The man had a net.

3. How did Ant save Dove?
   - Ⓐ Ant gave Dove a leaf.
   - Ⓑ Ant gave the man a net.
   - ● Ant bit the man's leg.

4. Why did Ant and Dove help each other?
   - Ⓐ They wanted to swim.
   - ● They are friends.
   - Ⓒ They were in a net.

104   The Ant and the Dove   Leveled Readers' Theater • EMC 3481 • © Evan-Moor Corp.

Page 105

Vocabulary Activity

Name _____

I Know the Words

Fill in the circle next to the correct answer.

1. You can swim _____.
   - Ⓐ in a net
   - ● in water
   - Ⓒ on a leaf

2. You stand on your _____.
   - ● leg
   - Ⓑ leaf
   - Ⓒ fly

3. You can catch a dove with _____.
   - Ⓐ water
   - ● a net
   - Ⓒ a leaf

4. You say "ouch" when you _____.
   - Ⓐ fly
   - Ⓑ swim
   - ● get hurt

5. To **grab** means to _____.
   - ● hold onto
   - Ⓑ fly
   - Ⓒ drink

© Evan-Moor Corp. • EMC 3481 • Leveled Readers' Theater   The Ant and the Dove   105

Page 106

Comprehension Activity

Name _____

I Know What Happened

Cut out the pictures. Glue them in order to show what happened in the play.

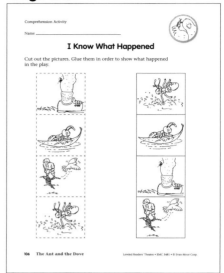

106   The Ant and the Dove   Leveled Readers' Theater • EMC 3481 • © Evan-Moor Corp.

Page 116

Comprehension Activity

Name _____

About the Play

Fill in the circle next to the correct answer.

1. What can you do in winter?
   - Ⓐ play in the water
   - ● play in the snow
   - Ⓒ look at eggs in a nest

2. What can you do in spring?
   - Ⓐ play in the leaves
   - Ⓑ play in the snow
   - ● look at eggs in a nest

3. What can you do in summer?
   - ● play in the water
   - Ⓑ play in the snow
   - Ⓒ look at eggs in a nest

4. What can you do in fall?
   - ● play in the leaves
   - Ⓑ play in the snow
   - Ⓒ look at eggs in a nest

116   Fun All Year   Leveled Readers' Theater • EMC 3481 • © Evan-Moor Corp.

Page 117

Vocabulary Activity

Name _____

I Know the Words

Fill in the circle next to the correct answer.

1. Snow falls in _____.
   - Ⓐ summer
   - ● winter
   - Ⓒ fall

2. Baby birds are born in _____.
   - Ⓐ fall
   - ● spring
   - Ⓒ winter

3. Leaves fall off a _____.
   - ● tree
   - Ⓑ horse
   - Ⓒ nest

4. You can see baby birds in _____.
   - Ⓐ water
   - ● a nest
   - Ⓒ snow

5. You can ride _____.
   - Ⓐ a bird
   - ● a horse
   - Ⓒ an egg

6. You can play in the _____.
   - Ⓐ birds
   - Ⓑ eggs
   - ● water

© Evan-Moor Corp. • EMC 3481 • Leveled Readers' Theater   Fun All Year   117

Page 118

Comprehension Activity

Name _____

Picture It

Follow the directions to draw the pictures.

1. Draw a tree with snow on it.

Drawings will vary.

2. Draw a tree that has a lot of leaves.

3. Draw a bird's nest in a tree.

118   Fun All Year   Leveled Readers' Theater • EMC 3481 • © Evan-Moor Corp.

Page 128

Comprehension Activity

Name _____

About the Play

Fill in the circle next to the correct answer.

1. Who had to watch the sheep?
   - Ⓐ the farmers
   - Ⓑ the wolf
   - ● the boy

2. What happened the first time the boy rang the bell and yelled?
   - ● The farmers came to help.
   - Ⓑ A wolf ate the sheep.
   - Ⓒ No one came to help.

3. What happened the last time the boy rang the bell and yelled?
   - Ⓐ The farmers came to help.
   - Ⓑ A wolf ate the sheep.
   - ● No one came to help.

4. Who tricked the boy?
   - ● the farmers
   - Ⓑ his father
   - Ⓒ the sheep

128   The Boy Who Yelled Wolf   Leveled Readers' Theater • EMC 3481 • © Evan-Moor Corp.

Page 129

Vocabulary Activity

Name _____

I Know the Words

Fill in the circle next to the correct answer.

1. Sheep eat _____.
   - ● grass
   - Ⓑ bells
   - Ⓒ farmers

2. You ring a _____.
   - Ⓐ boy
   - Ⓑ wolf
   - ● bell

3. If you need help, you _____.
   - Ⓐ eat
   - ● yell
   - Ⓒ play a trick

4. You hear a bell _____.
   - Ⓐ yell
   - Ⓑ play a trick
   - ● ring

5. You run up a _____.
   - ● hill
   - Ⓑ ring
   - Ⓒ sheep

© Evan-Moor Corp. • EMC 3481 • Leveled Readers' Theater   The Boy Who Yelled Wolf   129

Page 130

Comprehension Activity

Name _____

I Know What Happened

Cut out the pictures. Glue them in order to show what happened in the play.

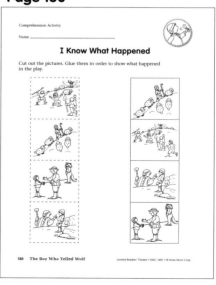

130   The Boy Who Yelled Wolf   Leveled Readers' Theater • EMC 3481 • © Evan-Moor Corp.

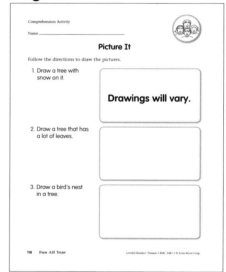
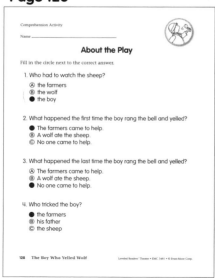
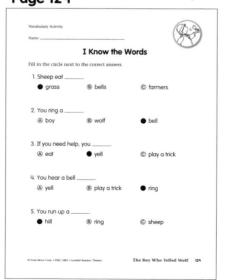

Page 140

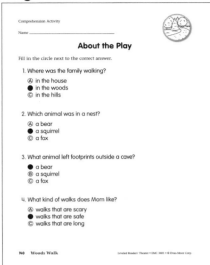

Comprehension Activity

Name _____

About the Play

Fill in the circle next to the correct answer.

1. Where was the family walking?
   - Ⓐ in the house
   - ● in the woods
   - Ⓒ in the hills

2. Which animal was in a nest?
   - Ⓐ a bear
   - ● a squirrel
   - Ⓒ a fox

3. What animal left footprints outside a cave?
   - ● a bear
   - Ⓑ a squirrel
   - Ⓒ a fox

4. What kind of walks does Mom like?
   - Ⓐ walks that are scary
   - ● walks that are safe
   - Ⓒ walks that are long

140   Woods Walk   Leveled Readers' Theater • EMC 3481 • © Evan-Moor Corp.

Page 141

Vocabulary Activity

Name _____

I Know the Words

Fill in the circle next to the correct answer.

1. A squirrel is _____.
   - ● an animal   Ⓑ a log   Ⓒ a flower

2. A den is _____.
   - Ⓐ an animal   Ⓑ a log   ● an animal's home

3. A fox makes a _____.
   - Ⓐ flower   ● den   Ⓒ nest

4. A bear's den may be _____.
   - ● in a cave   Ⓑ in a nest   Ⓒ in a log

5. You can walk in _____.
   - ● woods   Ⓑ nests   Ⓒ logs

© Evan-Moor Corp. • EMC 3481 • Leveled Readers' Theater   Woods Walk   141

Page 142

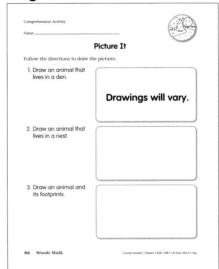

Comprehension Activity

Name _____

Picture It

Follow the directions to draw the pictures.

1. Draw an animal that lives in a den.

Drawings will vary.

2. Draw an animal that lives in a nest.

3. Draw an animal and its footprints.

142   Woods Walk   Leveled Readers' Theater • EMC 3481 • © Evan-Moor Corp.

Page 152

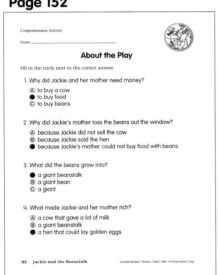

Comprehension Activity

Name _____

About the Play

Fill in the circle next to the correct answer.

1. Why did Jackie and her mother need money?
   - Ⓐ to buy a cow
   - ● to buy food
   - Ⓒ to buy beans

2. Why did Jackie's mother toss the beans out the window?
   - Ⓐ because Jackie did not sell the cow
   - Ⓑ because Jackie sold the hen
   - ● because Jackie's mother could not buy food with beans

3. What did the beans grow into?
   - ● a giant beanstalk
   - Ⓑ a giant bean
   - Ⓒ a giant

4. What made Jackie and her mother rich?
   - Ⓐ a cow that gave a lot of milk
   - Ⓑ a giant beanstalk
   - ● a hen that could lay golden eggs

152   Jackie and the Beanstalk   Leveled Readers' Theater • EMC 3481 • © Evan-Moor Corp.

Page 153

Vocabulary Activity

Name _____

I Know the Words

Fill in the circle next to the correct answer.

1. Beans can grow into a _____.
   - Ⓐ girl   ● beanstalk   Ⓒ giant

2. You can buy food with _____.
   - Ⓐ beans   Ⓑ a hen   ● money

3. You eat _____.
   - ● soup   Ⓑ money   Ⓒ a man

4. Clouds are in the _____.
   - Ⓐ window   Ⓑ house   ● sky

5. If you did it one time, you did it _____.
   - ● once   Ⓑ always   Ⓒ never

6. A giant is a very _____.
   - ● big person   Ⓑ small person   Ⓒ tiny bird

© Evan-Moor Corp. • EMC 3481 • Leveled Readers' Theater   Jackie and the Beanstalk   153

Page 154

Comprehension Activity

Name _____

I Know What Happened

Cut out the pictures. Glue them in order to show what happened in the play.

154   Jackie and the Beanstalk   Leveled Readers' Theater • EMC 3481 • © Evan-Moor Corp.

Read and Understand

The perfect comprehensive resource to supplement your core reading program! Motivating reading selections accompanied by comprehension and vocabulary activities make *Read and Understand* a must-have resource for providing students with extra reading practice and test prep. 144 pages. ***Correlated to state standards.***

Each Read and Understand *title includes:*

- *19 to 23 reproducible stories or poems*
- *multiple activity pages to practice comprehension, vocabulary, and other vital language arts skills*
- *engaging illustrations that support the text*

Story pages

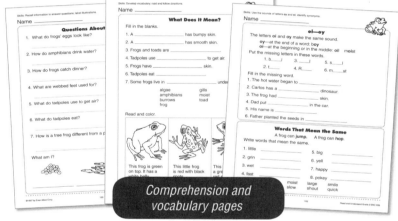

Comprehension and vocabulary pages

Read and Understand Stories and Activities

Grade K	EMC 637-PRO
Grade 1	EMC 638-PRO
Grade 2	EMC 639-PRO
Grade 3	EMC 640-PRO

Fiction
Grades 4–6+	EMC 748-PRO

Nonfiction
Grades 4–6+	EMC 749-PRO

More Read and Understand Stories and Activities

Grade 1	EMC 745-PRO
Grade 2	EMC 746-PRO
Grade 3	EMC 747-PRO

Read and Understand Poetry

Grades 2–3	EMC 3323-PRO
Grades 3–4	EMC 3324-PRO
Grades 4–5	EMC 3325-PRO
Grades 5–6+	EMC 3326-PRO

Read and Understand Literature Genres

Fairy Tales & Folktales
Grades 1–2	EMC 756-PRO

Folktales & Fables
Grades 2–3	EMC 757-PRO

Tall Tales
Grades 3–4	EMC 758-PRO

Myths & Legends
Grades 4–6+	EMC 759-PRO

Read and Understand Science

Grades 1–2	EMC 3302-PRO
Grades 2–3	EMC 3303-PRO
Grades 3–4	EMC 3304-PRO
Grades 4–6+	EMC 3305-PRO

Preview at
www.evan-moor.com